Dead Man's Axe

Guitar Store Mysteries, vol. 1

Bing Turkby

Guitarmerston North

First published in 2022 by

Guitarmerston North Books

Palmerston North

Aotearoa / New Zealand

Copyright © 2022 Bing Turkby

All rights reserved.

ISBN (Paperback): 978-0-473-62077-6

ISBN (ebook): 978-0-473-62150-6

ISBN (Kindle): 978-0-473-62078-3

Cover art and design by Jeroen ten Berge

The moral right of the author has been asserted.

Dead Man's Axe

CHAPTER 1

The day was as bright and beautiful as a Jimi Hendrix guitar solo, and Paws McCartney was a happy guitar shop cat. The old black and white furburger had cunningly found the place where he was least likely to be interrupted. He lay curled atop the cash register in a dust-speckled shaft of afternoon sunlight.

Dana – the owner of the Pick Me Guitar Shop, and Paws' human factotum – contemplated rousing the cat so she could tally up, but the register was often depressingly empty these days, so it probably wasn't worth it.

A piece of paper poked out from under Paws' furry tummy. Dana couldn't quite remember what it was, but she knew she had put it there this morning to remind her of something.

She looked over to where young Brody was caressing an expensive guitar. Ostensibly, he was dusting it. If only she could convince him to show the customers that much attention, she'd be rich.

Brody had been working at the store almost since she'd opened it three years ago. Back then, he'd come in every day after school. Now he'd graduated, with an A in daydreaming and an F in paying attention, and the shop was really all he had.

Dana knew she should probably let Brody go, but dammit, she couldn't fire him, no matter how tight the finances were. In small-to-medium-town Aotearoa, there wasn't a whole orchestra of options available to a young, semi-committed musician.

And the town of Rockingham West – named after a British politician from the 1700s, of all things – was quintessentially small-to-medium-town Aotearoa. To be fair, "Rock West", as the locals were sometimes inclined to call it, was larger than the original town of Rockingham, over the strait, on the east coast of the island Te Waipounamu. But that was hardly a claim that covered both towns in glory.

Naming places after politicians from a country they'd fled for a better life seems to have been a national obsession for early Pākehā in Aotearoa. Even though the places had already been named by Māori who'd been there for centuries.

While Dana pondered all of that, her gaze went to the wall above the counter, where a photo of her brother Ziggy was on prominent display. He beamed down at her from the picture frame, guitar in hand, legs splayed as he stood in front of a wall of Marshall amplifiers.

Though there was a family resemblance between them in many ways – the hazel eyes, the cheeky grin they both often displayed – there were just as many differences. Ziggy had the long flowing golden locks of a stadium rocker, always dressed in black, and had sunglasses semi-permanently glued to his face. While Dana, the high-energy punk/funk devotee, kept her short hair in various colours, and favoured bright clothes with bold patterns. However, despite those appearances, Ziggy had always been an extrovert. Loved being surrounded by people. In contrast, Dana just needed her cat, her bed and a stack of good books, and she was in heaven.

And, of course, there was a much bigger difference between them, now. Dana was upright and breathing, whereas poor Ziggy...

'He would've been proud of you, huh?'

Dana jumped as Brody's voice sounded right behind her. She hadn't noticed him move.

'Sorry, what was that?' she said.

'He'd be proud,' repeated Brody, nodding at the photo, 'of you owning a guitar shop.'

It wasn't the first time Brody had made this observation, and Dana supposed it wouldn't be the last either. She appreciated the sentiment behind it, but it did rather ignore the fact that Dana was an accomplished guitarist in her own right. Though she'd never toured with a popular band like Ziggy was doing before his untimely death, and she was known for preferring the brutal simplicity of punk songs, Dana actually possessed a better knowledge of music theory than Ziggy had, and could improvise over tricky jazz changes with the best of them. She was beginning to build up a roster of students, in her practice room above the shop.

So it's not as though she started the shop simply as a shrine to Ziggy's memory.

Okay, it may have been part of the reason.

One voice, but not the whole chorus.

Not wanting to hash through all of that tonight, she just said, 'Yes, Brody, I like to think he'd be proud.'

Dana was looking forward to turning off the lights, shooing Brody out the door, then heading to her flat upstairs so she could finish the book she was halfway through. The sun was disappearing and a chill was creeping in, so she couldn't wait to snuggle down for a good read. Paws McCartney would be looking forward to his dinner too.

But Brody wasn't finished yet.

'Ziggy would've probably wanted to come out

with us tonight, too, huh?'

Aaaaaah… Now Dana remembered about the piece of paper that Paws was sleeping on. It was a flyer for a gig. A gig that she'd promised to accompany Brody to, a few days ago. Oh, how her aching feet protested the folly of that moment of weakness.

Also, Dana was dubious that her famous musician brother would've joined them to watch a local pub gig with performances provided by some of her less talented, but more enthusiastic students. Although, actually, yeah, he might have really dug it.

'Um, you sure you still wanna go to that?' asked Dana.

'Oh hell yeah!' said Brody, whipping off his sweater to proudly display a bright yellow t-shirt emblazoned with the logo of the band This Plastic Happiness, a local goth/post-punk group. 'Evan will totally notice me wearing this, right?'

'Sure,' replied Dana, 'I guess.'

Brody's face fell.

'No, of course he will, Brodes. I just think that, you know, you went to school with him for five years and never spoke a word to him. Maybe you could try, actually, well... talking to him next time he comes into the shop. Or something.'

Evan from This Plastic Happiness came into Pick Me for bass strings quite often. Suspiciously often, in fact. Most bass players Dana knew only changed their strings when they went rusty and became a health hazard. Some bassists continued to play on even then, judging septicaemia an acceptable price to pay to achieve a deep, fat bass tone.

It was plain that Evan and Brody both liked each other, and Dana really hoped they'd get together, but what did her thirty-mumble-year-old self know about playing matchmaker to two twenty-year-old guys?

Oh no, she was staying well out of that.

Except, oh yes, she had agreed to go to the gig tonight and basically be Brody's wing-woman. The whole idea was terrifying and embarrassing and she couldn't imagine what she'd been thinking when she agreed to it.

The only upside was that one of the other bands on the bill was Audible Marks. This was a new band that everybody was raving about, and Dana was especially keen to see the guitarist, Nikau, who had been taking lessons from a guy called Gene Stevens.

Dana had met Stevens at many guitar-related events over the years, and he had always been brusque, if not downright rude, to her. He often dragged his son along to trade shows and made him perform for people, as if bullying your son into playing well was a good advertisement for a guitar teacher. Stevens was a lawyer who also played guitar, which, to a guitar shop owner, was the same thing as saying 'money tree'. Except, unfortunately for Dana, Stevens lived on the other side of town in a swanky house, and would never be seen dead in her neighbourhood. So all of his guitar money went to the big chain store Guitarz Guitars – her closest competition, over in Allendale, a much bigger city about an hour's drive away. It was bad enough that they attracted most of her little town's guitar customers, while she could barely pay rent. But the thing that Dana really couldn't stand was losing out to a shop that had a 'z' instead of an 's' in its name.

People with cash who wanted to see more options headed to places like Guitarz Guitars. Or, if the customer was especially flush, they might venture into Zander's Rare Guitars, where the wealthy collectors waved their wallets.

At the other end of the spectrum was Meltdown Music, where a haphazard collection of cheap and cheerful instruments lurked in dimly-lit corners. If a buyer didn't mind a few dings and scrapes, they could be assured of finding a guitar-shaped item that made guitar-like noises for very little outlay.

Brody shuffled his feet and mumbled something about checking the stock in the back room.

Dana shooed the cat off the till and fished out the moth-eaten float, flicked off the lights, and went to find a warm coat for the walk to the venue. She envied Paws McCartney, staying in the nice cosy flat while she went out.

***

As she and Brody made their way to the gig, Dana reflected that the only difference between Brody and her regular customers was that he wore a name badge and the others didn't. They all sat around picking on guitars and swapping tall stories. Talked about their mythical best gigs from back in the day; semi-famous bands they'd supported; tours they might have gone on if it hadn't been for the damn singer deciding to go solo at just that particular time.

If any one of them had actually bought a guitar, Dana would have died of shock.

That wasn't fair, really. Her regulars bought strings and accessories in enough quantity to keep things ticking over, they just didn't always have the cash for the big-ticket purchases like high-end guitars, and hand-wired amplifiers.

But every so often the shop got a fiscal shot in the arm from a moneyed-up customer, the kind she saw very irregularly indeed. Some of those people didn't even care about discounts – didn't even ask sometimes.

Dana had to suppress another sigh. Imagine. Not even caring whether you could get a discount on something. What must that be like? To buy a big-ticket item, and just swish your card through without asking for ten percent off. Crumpling your receipt into your pocket without carefully checking it for errors.

Years ago, Dana had worked at a cheap restaurant with a guy who claimed he didn't even know which week was pay week, because there was always money in his bank account. Dana had been astonished. Stood there like a cartoon character, with her mouth literally hanging open. I mean, the guy had bills, like anyone else. But he said he just never spent money on anything, so there was always enough in his account and he didn't have to check before, say, going to the grocery store.

Dana was so jealous. She had to check under the driver's seat for loose change before paying for parking.

And now that she owned a guitar shop, it was even worse. Thank goodness she lived above the shop and never went anywhere…

Well, except for tonight.

As she trudged next to Brody with her hands tucked into her armpits, a vexatious breeze tried to tug her beanie off her head. This had better be a really good gig.

CHAPTER 2

Dana paid the door charge at The Riffery, and got her wrist stamped. Having gained entrance to the venue's hallowed portal, she looked back and saw that Brody was just standing there, moving his weight from one foot to the other like a nervous backup singer, and giving her a pleading look.

She rolled her eyes and fished some more cash out of her purse. There goes that cut and dye she'd been looking forward to.

As they pushed their way through the heavy doors, the music suddenly leapt up in volume. Heck, if this was just the background music, how loud were the bands going to be? Had gigs always been this loud? Or is this just what getting old was like?

She popped her earplugs in. Never went anywhere without them, now. Seriously, anywhere. Dana knew too many people with tinnitus. She would hate to be subjected to the constant ringing in her ears. And there was a bonus to using plugs: sometimes a mix sounded better with them in. Cut down any harsh frequencies in the room. Like tonight's venue: literally a large brick box, awash with reverb. Most of the high frequencies were being soaked up by the people in the room, though, so that was good.

Dana used a little more of her cash-hoard grabbing a beer from the bar. At least Brody was sticking with water, free from the filtered tap.

A couple of people recognised her and gave her a nod. They might have talked about guitars with her but it was too loud to do much of that.

A person she didn't know nudged their friend and pointed at her. She could see Ziggy's name on their lips.

She'd had to get used to this from a young age, with Ziggy being such a precocious talent. But now it had a jagged edge to it. She was no longer 'that cool guitarist's sister', but now 'that dead guitarist's sister'.

It hurt. But, it wasn't going to get any less hurtful, so she just had to get on with her life.

This Plastic Happiness took to the stage to scattered applause. And a deafening whistle from Brody. The bass player, Evan, spotted Brody's t-shirt and gave him a thumbs-up before they kicked off their first song.

Brody was ecstatic. He jumped up and down in front of the stage for their whole set, even though the band's gloom-laden electro-plod was not intended for such a purpose, and nobody else in the whole place joined in.

They played a pretty good set, though. Especially their last song: Dead For Life. Okay, maybe the lyrics and song title could do with some polishing, but overall it was a good song, with a strong, hummable melody and a cool syncopated rhythm. She was also pleased to note that her student Amelie acquitted herself well on guitar. The young woman had obviously been putting in good practice time.

Hopefully the band would stick at it and keep improving. So many bands imploded before they actually got good enough to make it worth staying together.

Dana used the fifteen-minute changeover break between bands to go to the ladies' room. She turned down the offer of a drink on the way back, from a guy doing some frankly mortifying dance moves near the mixing desk. She found herself grateful to be out with someone to accompany her, even if it was only Brody, so that she didn't have to fend off the guy's unwanted attention all night.

By the time she got back to her spot near the mixing desk, Audible Marks had started their set. Brody was no longer front and centre. He was now – completely coincidentally, of course – over by the far wall, in line of sight of the door to the bands' green room. Just in case a certain bass player should emerge.

Audible Marks were a new band but most of the members were Dana's age. They'd recruited the much younger Nikau as their guitar player, and she could see why. From the first song, Dana was impressed with him. Either the kid was a genius, or Gene Stevens was a miraculously good teacher. Maybe both. Say what you will about Gene's grumpiness, he was obviously doing something right with Nikau.

The rest of the band were good, but they weren't on Nikau's level. Dana could see him holding back sometimes, just trying to keep the band together by playing simple, steady chords. Every so often, if the song called for it, he would insert some shimmering arpeggios, or the odd concise, well-composed lead break. The fact that he knew when to keep it steady and when to pour on the juice impressed Dana. Most guitarists had a desperate need to show the audience exactly how many cool licks they knew, throwing them in even when they ruined a song.

'Wow, they've got some flash guitars, these people.'

Great. The guy with the bad dance moves had strutted his way over, and was trying to have a conversation with her over the loud music.

'That last band were all playing cheap rubbish,' the guy continued, half-shouting as he kept up his jerky movements. 'But, believe it or not, that guitarist,' he sloshed his drink towards Nikau, 'is playing an instrument worth thousands. It's a Draydon Weka. Ever heard of that?'

Dana resisted the impulse to slap her hand against her forehead. Then she resisted a second impulse, this time to slap the bad dancer's mansplaining cakehole.

'No way it's a real Weka,' Dana replied in a shout of her own. 'It must be a Bluff.'

Jerky Dancing Guy lost all coordination and almost spilled the rest of his drink as he eyed Dana with surprise.

'You know about Bluffs?'

Dana wasn't about to lose her voice trying to prove her credentials to this cretin. So she simply said 'Yes,' and let the current of the dancing crowd drag her away.

Most people at the gig would probably have heard about the famous guitar the Draydon Weka,

Dana reflected as she shimmied her way to a stool at the bar. And, since a significant proportion of people who attended gigs were musicians themselves, many of them would also know about fake versions of those guitars, called Bluffs.

The Draydon company had produced several hundred of their Weka model guitar in the early Sixties. There weren't many left now, and those that were still extant were often locked away in collections. A sharp-eyed buyer could still find one if they were patient, but one of those would definitely be out of young Nikau's price range.

The standard version was simply called the Weka, and there was also a blinged-up version called the Buff Weka, with gold hardware, and fancy binding on the body. They looked and played like a million dollars, sometimes literally. But since the two versions had the same main ingredients, they were both highly desirable instruments. People said there was a special magic to the way they wound the pickups on those guitars. And the wood - oh! That specific type of wood was unobtainable nowadays. Illegal to log it, sell it, strum it.

Which is why the market was currently flooded with hundreds, if not thousands, of cheap copies of the Draydon guitar. It had gotten so bad there was even a generic name for a copy of that specific guitar - a Bluff Weka. See, musicians can be funny, Dana thought.

So, Nikau's Bluff was no doubt a good enough instrument, but nothing anywhere near as eye-wateringly expensive as the bass player's birds-eye maple five-string, or his towering vintage bass amp.

Still, Jerky Dancing Guy's condescension rankled Dana. There was nothing wrong with cheaper instruments these days, and no shame in rocking one. Also, he shouldn't be so surprised that a female might know this.

There was only so long that Dana could spend ogling expensive musical instruments, especially since she spent most of her day staring at the ones hanging, unsold, on her walls. Having listened to three songs from Audible Marks, she'd heard enough to know they were worth keeping an eye on, but now it was definitely approaching cocoa-and-book-in-bed time.

Stifling a yawn, Dana spotted Evan the bass player exiting the green room door. She watched him make his way over to compliment Brody on his choice of t-shirt.

Dana raised an eyebrow at Brody, and he nodded back, so that was her cue to leave.

Outside, it was blissfully fresh after being in the

hot sweaty club, so Dana didn't mind waiting a few minutes for a cab.

CHAPTER 3

The next day was another quiet one, customer-wise, but Brody filled the gaps by talking non-stop about hanging out with Evan the night before. Dana didn't feel a burning desire to hear all the details, but she was pleased to hear him so happy.

If she was being honest, one of the main reasons Dana could never fire Brody is that he reminded her of Ziggy. Like Brody, her brother would happily chatter away to anyone who drifted close enough.

The day passed slowly but it got there in the end. As Brody flipped the closed sign, eager to head off and meet up with a certain bass player, he spotted a customer coming up to the door. Terrified that he'd be late for his date, he fled out the back, hoping the customer hadn't seen him and would just leave. As he scuttled through the shop, he scared Paws McCartney off his latest cosy spot on top of the effect pedal display stand, and left Dana stranded in the middle of cashing up.

'Sorry, we're closed,' yelled Dana, staying where she was at the till.

'Please!' came the muffled response from outside. The guy was persistent, she'd give him that. 'I just need some strings for a gig tonight.'

Dana's shoulders slumped. She was never going to say no to that. For one thing, she could do with the sale, no matter how small. For another, she could never let a fellow musician down. If someone had a gig and needed strings, she would have got up out of bed at any hour to help out.

You do for family. And Dana considered all Rockingham West musicians to be part of one big family.

She trudged back over to the door, and let the guy in.

'Thanks,' he said. 'I usually have spare sets, but my nephew's been staying with me, and he must've grabbed my stash, the cheeky little shit.'

Dana smiled, and looked at the photo of Ziggy out of the corner of her eye. Oh yes, she knew all about that kind of situation.

'Come on in. Electric guitar strings, is it? Or acoustic?'

'Electric, thanks.'

'What string gauge do you use? Nines?' She raised an eyebrow. 'Or are you one of those masochists who likes twelves?'

Dana always found it amusing that some guitarists used the thickness of their guitar string gauge as a flex over other guitarists. Honestly, just use the strings you like, people. If you enjoy playing heavier strings then just do it, you don't get extra points for banging on about it. Also, some of the best players in the world used lighter strings, and you didn't hear their fans complaining.

The customer laughed, obviously of the same opinion as Dana. 'Nines are a bit too light for me, but twelves are way too heavy. Tens will do me just fine. Do you have a ten-to-forty-six set?'

'Sure do,' said Dana, walking over to the wall of strings behind the counter. 'Set of three is cheaper in the long run.'

'Set of three it is, then.' The guy plopped his wallet on the counter and laughed again. 'Not that I plan on breaking any tonight, but I feel better knowing I have spares.'

'I hear ya. The day you don't take spares is the day you really need 'em. Am I right?'

'Hell yes. I also take a spare guitar, and even a spare amp too.' He shrugged. 'I'm probably a touch paranoid, I suppose you could say.'

'Are you kidding me? When you can fit a lunchbox amp in your glovebox, you'd be crazy not to take a spare.'

As Dana rang up the sale, the guy's eyes ranged around the shop, with its eclectic collections of posters, flyers and album covers. Dana could almost feel the weight of the next statement coming out of his mouth. So she beat him to it.

'Yes, Ziggy was my brother.'

'Oh,' said the guy, taken aback. 'Yeah, I thought so.' He pointed to a guitar lessons flyer. 'But I was gonna ask: You're the one who gives the lessons, right?'

Dana flushed. 'Yes. Sorry, people always ask me about Ziggy.'

'No need to apologise.' He waved it away. 'That must get annoying.'

She handed him his strings. 'Well, yeah, it can be annoying. And it also makes me sad. But...' she shrugged. 'I mean, it's nice that so many people thought so highly of him, you know?'

He smiled, and nodded. 'Well, anyway. If you're anywhere near as good as he was, I'd love to sign up for lessons with you.'

'You're good enough to be out gigging, and you still want to take lessons? I'm impressed.' Dana honestly meant that. She knew of several gigging musicians who could actually do with a few lessons to tidy up their playing, or at least some more focused practice time. Most would never deign to do so, as if it was an admission of failure.

'If it was good enough for Randy Rhoads, it's good enough for me,' said the customer. 'That guy kept taking lessons even as he was on the road, touring.'

'You can always learn more, that's for sure.' She smiled. 'I wish I had more students like you. I'm tempted to kick a couple out just to accommodate you.' She laughed. 'But seriously, let me have a look at my diary and I'll let you know.'

'Thanks. I'm Rawiri, by the way.' His smile faded as he continued. 'I was getting lessons from Gene Stevens, you see. But obviously not any more.'

'Why obviously?'

'You haven't heard?'

'Heard what?'

'Ah, it sucks…' Rawiri winced, and sucked in a breath between his teeth. 'He was murdered.'

Dana's hand flew to her chest. 'Murdered? Oh my god!'

'Yeah, in his own home. Look.' Rawiri called up a news report on his phone for her.

Music teacher takes his last bow, the headline blared.

'Sweet mercy,' said Dana. 'The poor guy.' She screwed up her nose. 'And surely they could have come up with a better title than that.'

'Yeah, it's pretty rank. Um, sorry, I really need to get going.' He slid his phone back into his pocket. 'Let me know if you have a space open up for me, yeah?'

'Will do, Rawiri. And thanks for letting me know about Gene. I'm sorry if you and him were close.'

'I didn't know him all that well, actually. I'd only been to a few lessons from him in the last month. But still, it's freaky.'

'For sure.' Dana was thankful, in a way, that Rawiri hadn't been close to Gene. She would have had to manufacture some sympathy for the irascible old guitar teacher. Even though she didn't wish him harm, she could understand why someone might have gotten offside with him.

'Anyway, thanks for the strings,' said Rawiri.

'No problem. Bye.'

Dana called up the news article on her laptop, and Paws McCartney slunk back into the room so he could walk back and forth over the keyboard as she tried to read.

The article included a brief speculation about why Gene had been killed. A few of his belongings had been taken, but nothing terribly valuable. In fact, the murderer had brained Gene with his own guitar, and then left it on the floor next to him.

Dana gasped. She knew for a fact that Gene's guitar was an actual 1961 Draydon Weka, the original version of the instrument she'd seen onstage last night with Nikau. Gene's Weka was worth somewhere in the neighbourhood of quarter to half a million dollars. It was one of those ultra-rare, uber-desirable instruments, almost like a Stradivarius violin. Surely the killer hadn't used that?

'Whooah!' breathed a voice at her shoulder.

Dana jumped about a foot in the air. 'Jesus! Brody! You're still here? Why the hell did you sneak up on me like that?'

Brody's face went red. 'Sorry, boss. I thought you heard me come through the door.'

Dana's heart rate slowly recalibrated itself, like a metronome that's taken a knock. 'It's okay.' She breathed out, hard. 'I'm sorry I yelled at you. You just scared me.'

As she calmed herself, they both read through the article. At the bottom was a photo of the crime scene. Dana zoomed in. There, in the corner of the room, was the Draydon guitar. Lying on the floor like it was just some old piece of wood. And the lower bout was covered in blood. Dana sucked on her teeth. This was sacrilege.

She frowned.

'There's something about that guitar,' she said.

'I'll say,' Brody replied. 'It's gorgeous. Supposedly it plays like a dream, too'

'Brody!' She slapped his arm. 'That's not what I meant,' she said. 'There's something… niggling at me about it.'

'Like, why would someone kill a person if not to steal a really nice guitar?'

'Well, there's definitely that to consider. But there's something else I can't quite put my finger on.' She sighed. 'What a tragedy, though. Gene was a great teacher, even if he wasn't the nicest guy.'

'Oh yeah,' said Brody, slouching against the counter. 'Actually, I heard he would sometimes give his students free strings if they couldn't afford them. Like, he came across as a horrible dark cloud, but sometimes a little sun would shine through.'

'Giving away strings for free.' Dana gave a wry chuckle. 'No wonder our shop's going out of business then, huh?'

Brody choked. 'We're going out of business?'

'Figure of speech, Brodes,' she held up her hands. 'Just a figure of speech. Sorry.'

Brody shook his head and scurried off, and Dana followed Paws McCartney up to her flat. She went to bed, and although Paws curled up on top of her tummy and was soon sound asleep, Dana lay awake for a long time. Something about that guitar just kept nagging at her.

CHAPTER 4

'Fake!' Dana yelled as Brody entered the shop the next morning.

'Excuse me?' said Brody, in the process of throwing his jacket in the corner of the back room. 'I've just stepped in the door and you're saying I'm fake? Rude!'

'Not you,' said Dana. 'The guitar in the photo. It's a fake. It's not Gene's Weka. Someone stole his extremely valuable guitar and left a fake behind. See?' She turned her laptop so Brody could see.

'Ooooh, wow, really?' Brody zipped over to the counter. 'Sneaky! Wait – two things: One, have you been standing here in the same place all night? And two: how do you know the guitar's a fake?'

'I have not been here all night, no.' Dana patted her hair and straightened her blouse. 'Okay, most of the night, yes. I couldn't stop thinking about the guitar. And look.' She zoomed in on the photo and pointed at the guitar's headstock. 'The truss rod cover is wrong. It's the wrong shape, and has three screws, not two.'

'Is that a big deal?'

Dana leaned back so she could give Brody the full benefit of a disbelieving stare, one eyebrow raised. 'By Saint Hendrix's shaggy hairdo!' she swore. 'Have I not trained you properly? Of course it's a big deal. It can mean the difference between a five hundred dollar copy and a five hundred thousand dollar legit Draydon. Now, you know I love a good cheap guitar, but given that choice, which would you prefer?'

'Oof. Gotcha. But, like, is that really enough to prove it's a fake by itself?'

'It's definitely enough to make me want to look closer. It's hard to tell from this angle, but maybe the Draydon logo is slightly skewed too. And I'd want to check the control cavity wiring, and inspect the binding around the edge of the body, to be one hundred percent sure.' Dana tapped a finger on her chin.

Brody glanced from her, to the photo, and back to her. 'You're going to go and have a look at it, aren't you?'

Dana nodded, giving the appearance that he was helping her to make up her mind. 'Yes. I mean, the people investigating the murder will want to know if it's fake, right?'

'I guess, yeah.'

'Because, according to the article, at the moment it looks like the only things that were taken from the room were a box of guitar picks and an old MIDI keyboard controller.'

'So?'

'Well, they're not worth anything. So the police might be looking for a killer who just took a few random things afterwards to make it look like a burglary gone wrong.' Dana grabbed Brody's arm. 'But you and I know that a very valuable guitar was taken. Swapped, in fact. To throw the police off the trail and onto an incorrect one.' Dana's voice dropped to a whisper. 'This isn't a burglar trying to get away with murder. It's a murderer trying to get away with burglary. So, I'd better go and tell the police.'

'What, you're going now?'

'Yep. You're in charge of the shop, Brody.'

'Me? All by myself?' Brody's voice had gone up by half an octave by the end of that sentence.

'Sure! I trust you.'

'You do?'

Dana stopped to think about this. Brody was legally old enough to be in charge of the store by himself. He probably wouldn't break anything or set the place on fire. He also probably wouldn't sell anything. So it was a neutral good, and that was good enough for her.

'Absolutely, Brody!' she said, and gave him a double thumbs-up.

***

Twenty minutes later, Dana was at the Police station, completely failing to speak to someone about the guitar.

The guy at the front desk had dismissed her as a crank straight off the bat, and when she demanded to speak to someone higher up, it hadn't really improved the situation.

Now she was perched on a hard, uninviting chair in the waiting area. It was almost as though they were trying to discourage people from hanging around in there, she mused.

The smell of ammonia and desperation suffused the air, and the stark white walls reflected back all the people's nervousness at being there.

An officer emerged from a back room, carefully avoiding eye contact with anyone in the waiting area as he attempted to make it to a door on the other side of the room without being accosted. His body language screamed: I'm busy! Please do not interrupt me.

For a second Dana debated stopping him anyway, but her nerve ran out and she slumped into her chair in defeat.

'Do I know you from somewhere?' She turned to find the officer staring at her as he stood there with his hand halfway to the door behind her. 'Wait, aren't you Ziggy Zane's sister?'

For possibly the first time ever, this statement did not cause Dana to wilt and sigh in frustration. She smiled.

'Yes, I'm Dana. Hello!'

She leapt up to shake the officer's hand, startling him with her enthusiasm so that he almost dropped the papers he was holding.

'Oh, okay, hi,' he said. 'I'm Wade. I saw Ziggy play at the Green Man a while back. He was… wow, just mind-blowing! I was very sorry to hear he passed away.'

'Thank you, officer,' said Dana. 'That's nice of you to say.'

Officer Wade nodded, and then seemed to remember his papers, and the office door that was beckoning to him. 'Well, nice to meet you, Dana. I'd better be getting on.'

'Wait,' she pleaded, as he pushed open the door and shuffled halfway through. 'I really need to talk to someone, but the guy at the desk thinks I'm crazy.'

Wade stopped. Dana could see his shoulders slump, even though he was professional enough to try to hide it. He looked fondly at the door, then back at Dana.

'Ahh, talk to someone about what, exactly?' He said.

She blurted out her suspicion about the fake guitar, and watched as his resignation slowly turned to guarded interest.

'Wow, okay then,' he said. 'I think the detective in charge will want to hear about this.' He held up a finger, almost dropping his papers in the process. 'Wait here, I'll be back in a sec.' Then he shouldered his way through the door.

When he returned several minutes later, it was in the company of an imposing woman holding half a kebab. She was taller than Dana, and she filled out her uniform in a way that suggested it would be unwise to mess with her.

'This is Detective Mary Shaw,' said Wade. 'She's investigating the Stevens homicide.'

'You're Dana Zane?' demanded the detective, pointing the kebab at her.

'Yes... well, no, it's Dana Osborne actually. My brother used Zane as a stage name — '

'Sure.' The woman cut her off with a distracted nod. 'This had better be worth my time, Dana. I'm supposed to be on my lunch break, I have ten reports to write, and the Chief wants me in court in...' she checked her watch. 'One hour.' She softened a little. 'But Wade vouches for you, so you have two minutes. Go.'

'Ah... okay, right. Well, I saw the picture of the room that Gene Stevens was killed in —'

'They should never have printed that!' thundered Shaw. 'Our lawyers are gonna have a field day with that newspaper.'

'Yes, but, the thing is, the guitar in the photo isn't Gene's guitar.'

'Listen, Miss Zane... sorry, Miss Osborne. We have a comprehensive list of items in that room, and the items which are missing from that room, supplied by Stevens family. I'm told that the guitar is a collector's piece. So I'm sure that the family would have noticed if there was something wrong with it.'

'Actually, they might not have noticed,' Dana replied. 'That's my whole point. Those guitars are so valuable that people have been making fake versions for a long time. They've gotten very good at it. But this one has some tell-tale signs that make me think it's not the real thing.'

Dana quickly summarised her thoughts, reiterating that she would need to examine the guitar in person to confirm the hypothesis.

Detective Mary Shaw took a bite of her kebab and chewed contemplatively for a minute. She glanced at Wade, and he nodded a response to her unspoken question.

Shaw turned back to Dana. 'All right, I'll let you look at the guitar just in case you're right. You'll need to sign an official waiver in case you do something stupid, and…' she leaned in so close that Dana was accosted by the tang of garlic and chilli. 'If you do something stupid you'll ruin my whole homicide investigation. And I will not be pleased. Understood?'

Dana nodded meekly.

'Good. And you'll be accompanied by an officer at all times.'

Before Wade could back out through the door, Shaw grabbed his arm. 'This officer here, in fact. Wade, please escort the nice lady to Interview Room Three. I'll call the evidence room and have them bring up the guitar.'

CHAPTER 5

As Dana waited for the guitar to arrive, Wade paced the interview room and checked his watch every three seconds. He caught Dana watching him.

'Sorry,' he said. 'Nothing against you, or the case, but I have so much paperwork sitting on my desk to get through, it's just not funny. I bet it will have doubled in size by the time I get back, too. My colleagues will have noticed I'm not there, and will be sneaking a few things off their own report piles.'

'That's a bummer. Sorry to take up your time.'

'Oh, no, it's okay. In fact, it's nice of you to be helping us out with this. You know, not every person who sees something that looks a bit off comes to tell the police about it, believe it or not.' He gave a wry smile.

There was a knock at the door, and Wade yanked it open. In walked a guy with a guitar case, and a piece of paper. Wade went to grab the guitar, but the guy pulled it away from him.

'Not till you've signed this, mate. C'mon, you know the drill. You think I'd hand over a valuable piece of evidence and just hope you'll return it?'

As Wade grudgingly signed the form, the evidence room guy continued his complaint, seeming glad to have a new person to vent to, in the form of Dana.

'Honestly, I had to search the place from top to bottom last week cos some idiot left a tomahawk lying around in the basement and forgot he'd put it there. They needed it for a court case that afternoon. I keep telling them, follow the process and the process will look after you, but —'

'Okay, thanks Geoff,' said Wade, waving the piece of paper in his face and pushing him out of the room, snagging the guitar from him as he did. 'Good work. Love your dedication. Carry on.'

He shut the door and sighed. 'Sorry about that.'

Dana gave a what-can-you-do-really-it's-fine kind of shrug, but her attention was already fixed on the guitar case.

At moments like this she couldn't help but think of her brother.

At the end of the tour which made him a household name, he'd been found dead in a hotel room. To make it even worse, someone had stolen his guitar while he lay lifeless on the floor. So Dana didn't even have that instrument to remember him by. It's not the sole reason she became a guitar dealer — she was actually a very accomplished guitarist herself, after all — but she'd be lying if she said she didn't get her hopes up every time someone brought in a guitar to trade. She would take deep breaths to calm herself while they cracked the case, and then have to deal with the inevitable disappointment when it wasn't Ziggy's instrument inside.

Even though there was no chance that today's instrument could be his — Ziggy played a Fender Stratocaster, not a Draydon — the familiar old feeling still crept over her.

Shaking it off, she accepted the guitar case from Wade and laid it on the pockmarked table in the middle of the room.

Dana's guitar-nerd senses kicked in immediately. Just the look and feel of the threadbare case was enough to make any guitar fan's heart flutter. I'm an authentic old case, it said to her. Imagine what kind of cool old guitar I'm hiding inside! She laid her hands on the worn outer fabric with reverential care, allowed herself a moment to savour the vibe, then threw the catches and lifted the lid.

Immediately, her lip curled, in an involuntary action. The guitar lying in the funky old case had no business being there. Even though it was hard not to get distracted by the – urgh – spots of blood on the lower bout, she could tell straight away that it was not a genuine vintage instrument.

Sure, it had the right shape, the correct number of pickups, and so on. Someone had even taken the time to age the plastic parts so they'd gone yellowy-white, and the nickel-plated bridge was artfully tarnished. The body's finish had been worn away on the upper part where a player's arm would have brushed against it repeatedly. However, the wear wasn't… right.

'If you pop these on, you can pick it up if you want,' said Wade, handing her some blue rubber gloves. 'It's already been dusted for prints, and before you ask, the only ones on it were Gene's, so obviously the killer took precautions.'

She wrangled the gloves on, and flexed her fingers, ready for a proper examination.

'What do you think?' asked Wade.

In response, Dana picked up the guitar, slung the strap over her shoulder, and held the instrument as if she was playing it.

'Notice anything about the paint wear pattern?'

Wade looked for a minute and then shook his head.

'Watch my arm when I play it,' said Dana.

She strummed a few chords, and then raised an eyebrow at Wade.

'Oh,' he said, as he realised what she was getting at. 'The paint is worn off in the wrong place.'

'That's right. To get wear like this you'd have to play the guitar with your arm way further forward than it would naturally hang.' She took the guitar off and turned it over and around, to inspect it closer and catch the harsh industrial light the room provided. 'However, I think this wear was created by someone using sandpaper. It's not quite the right pattern for arm wear, you see? And you can juuuuust make out the circular sanding grooves, right at the edges.'

Wade nodded, although his eyebrows assumed a pose of mild confusion. 'Okay, but what if someone actually has been playing the guitar with their arm twisted forward like that? I mean, you could do that, couldn't you?'

'Sure,' said Dana. 'I mean, it's technically possible. It's just that we know Gene Stevens didn't play like that. And we also have photos of his original guitar from a few years ago, going right back to the eighties, and it never had that wear pattern.'

Wade whistled. 'Wow. You've done your homework on this.'

Dana nodded. 'It's my job. There are people out there who can identify a guitar based only on the striated patterns in the abalone fretboard inlays.' She smiled. 'I'm not one of them, but I know enough to tell you that this isn't Gene's guitar.'

'You're absolutely sure?'

Dana, absorbed in checking the binding around the body's edge, gave a distracted 'mmm-hmmm' in the affirmative.

'Look,' she said, pointing at the area where the neck joined the body. 'The end of the binding is supposed to match up exactly with this fret here, see? But it doesn't. It's sloppy work. Never would have left the factory if it was done in the late fifties. Also...' she peered closely at the headstock. 'I think this inlaid Draydon logo isn't made of abalone.'

Wade peered at it. 'I dunno, it looks like abalone.'

'That's the point, with a fake' said Dana, almost managing not to roll her eyes. 'I think it's mother of toilet seat.'

Wade made a sound halfway between a cough and a laugh, and had to pop out to the front desk to grab a tissue to clean himself up.

'You what?' he said when he returned.

'Sorry,' said Dana with a smile. 'I forget that guitarists have some weird in-jokes. Companies used to make fake mother of pearl out of plastic, and they would put it on all sorts of things: accordions, guitars, and…' she waited for Wade to catch on.

'Oh!' he said. 'I think I've seen an old toilet seat like that, in my nan's house.'

'There you go,' said Dana, making a voila kind of hand gesture towards the guitar's headstock. 'Mother of toilet seat. Now, I'll take a few photos, if that's alright, so I can do some more research at home?'

Wade gave a hesitant nod. 'Hmmm… okay. But you have to promise that you won't show them to anyone else.'

'Of course.'

She pulled her cellphone out of her bag and tried to photograph the instrument from every angle, moving it around to get the best light.

Then she put the guitar back in its case — no, not this guitar's own case, but the case of the actual vintage guitar, now confirmed missing — and sat down on a wobbly plastic chair.

'I bet,' she said, 'that if I looked in the control cavity under blacklight I'd find even more evidence, but this alone is enough. It's definitely not Gene's vintage Weka.'

Wade sat down heavily next to her. 'Right then.' He puffed out his cheeks. 'I think you've just established the motive for murder.'

CHAPTER 6

Wade packed up the guitar and took it back to Geoff in the evidence room, leaving Dana to write out a statement on her findings.

When he returned, he took her statement and ushered her back to the lobby.

'Thanks again, Miss Osborne. This has been really helpful.'

'Oh, um, no problem. I, ah…'

'Yes?'

'Well, it's just that I wondered…'

Wade gave her a suspicious look. 'You're not going to ask me to keep you in the loop on the case, are you?'

Dana's face went red.

'Because,' Wade continued, 'you're not a Police officer. You get that, right? Just because you've helped us with the investigation doesn't mean you're now on the payroll or anything.'

'Yeah. No, I get it,' mumbled Dana.

Wade softened. 'It's just that what happens is, a lot of people watch fluffy TV shows about amateur detectives, and then they think they're living in a TV show, and then they start to ask for updates as if they're the Chief Inspector. You're not one of those people, are you?' He raised an eyebrow. 'Are you?'

That last part came out as more of a statement than a question, and there was nothing Dana could do except shake her head in agreement and then flee out the front door, mortally embarrassed.

She crossed the street and sought refuge from her shame in a small park surrounding a stagnant pond.

She kicked a pebble into the pond, and summoned up a few curse words that Ziggy had taught her when they were kids.

Yes, actually, she damn well did want to be updated on the case! She was burning to find out who had killed Gene, and why, and what had happened to his guitar. And, if she was being honest with herself, not necessarily in that order.

She took a deep breath.

It's not about me, she told herself.

She wasn't expecting a reply, so was surprised when another voice in her head chimed in with: But it is about guitars, and you're the guitar guru.

That voice had a point, but Dana wasn't so egotistical as to subscribe to that way of thinking.

No. She adjusted the strap of her handbag on her shoulder, and stood up straight. Having successfully told herself off for getting too involved, she resolved to leave the sleuthing to the sleuths.

With that thought, she headed back to the store.

***

Brody was buzzing with excitement about Dana's encounter with law enforcement. He made her go over everything in minute detail. Then over it again every time a new customer entered the store, like a never-ending coda on a piece of music.

'Hush, Brody, they don't want to hear about all this stuff.'

'Are you kidding?' said Craig, one of their regulars, who spent almost as much time in the store as Dana did, but nowhere near as much money. 'This is huge! Do you realise what this means?'

'That a callous murderer killed Gene Stevens over a guitar?'

Craig paused for a second. 'Well, yes. That, of course. Which is horrible, of course. May he jam with Hendrix in the afterlife, and so on. But...' he held up a finger for emphasis. 'It also means that there's a gorgeous vintage Draydon out there in the wind somewhere.' His eyes got a glazed, faraway look as he stared out the front window. No doubt he was imagining himself finding said guitar for a bargain price at a local pawn shop.

Dana knew her customers well, and they were all good, upstanding citizens… unless you got between them and a guitar they desired. Then all bets were off.

She got a chill down the back of her neck. Surely nobody that she knew would have killed Gene, would they? No. It was unthinkable. There's a world of difference between haggling for a good price on an instrument, and killing someone for it.

No. She shook herself. None of her customers would do such a thing, no matter what bollocks they might talk about it in the store.

'So anyway,' said Brody, interrupting her sombre reflections. 'When do you think they'll get back to you about how the investigation is progressing? Will they call you in again soon, you reckon?'

She gave a condescending laugh, as if the very same thought had never occurred to her. 'Oh, Brody, don't be silly. They're under no obligation to keep me up to date with their progress. It's not like I'm the police chief, is it? Ha! No, that only happens on TV shows, not in real life. Honestly, Brodes…'

She shook her head at him, and then hastily

ducked behind the counter to tidy up the hanging bags of guitar strings.

Brody, chastened, slunk over to the main guitar display wall and began his usual daily routine of playing all the guitars, under the guise of checking they were in tune.

Craig, the customer, asked if he could plug a guitar into one of the new amps that had just arrived in stock. Dana nodded, and tossed him a guitar cable. She knew that Craig wouldn't be buying the amp, but she never minded him trying stuff out because he was careful with gear, never played too loud, and maybe just as importantly, it absolutely made his day. Running a guitar shop was more of a community service than a business, something Dana had found out the hard way. She'd never be rich, but usually she made enough to get by, and she got to hang out and talk music all day. She counted herself lucky.

Absorbed in her thoughts of contented penury, she was startled when her phone rang. She fished it out of her purse and checked the caller ID.

Huh. It was Wade, the policeman. Dana wondered if another guitar-related case had popped up.

'Hi, Wade. How can I help?'

'Oh, hi, Miss Osborne. I, ah, I actually have a

follow-up question about that guitar, if you don't mind?'

'Sure! No problem.' Dana waved to get Brody's attention, pointed to herself and then to the back room. She slipped through the door, and pushed some old guitar catalogues off a stool to perch on, since Paws McCartney was already firmly ensconced in the comfy office chair.

'Right,' said Wade. 'Detective Shaw read your statement, and was pleased you were able to tell us for sure that the guitar in Gene Stevens' house is not actually his original guitar. As I said earlier, it gives us a motive for his murder. Without that, we'd have been looking at a completely random attack, which is much harder to investigate.'

'Oh, well that's good then. Was there something else you needed me to check?'

'Not as such,' said Wade. 'But we're hoping we might make use of your specialist field of knowledge, and your local contacts.'

'Absolutely,' Dana replied immediately. 'Anything I can do to help.'

Wade cleared his throat. 'We'll be collecting statements from everybody who was at Gene's house on the day he was killed. That includes all of Gene's students, of course, plus his household.'

'Oh yes, he had a wife and… was it one child? A

boy?'

'That's right, Devon is his boy, and his wife is Maya. Devon is actually twenty-three years old.'

Wow. Reality check. Dana flashed back to seeing Gene and his little boy at a guitar educator's get-together. It seemed like only a couple of years ago but was obviously over a decade now.

'Miss Osborne, I wonder if you would mind...' Wade sighed, obviously struggling with the rest of the sentence. 'If you would mind accompanying us to the interviews. See if you can spot anything else that might be helpful.'

Dana couldn't help herself. 'So, you mean, you'd like to keep me in the loop on this case?'

'Haha. Yes. Very funny,' replied Wade in a monotone. He cleared his throat. 'I've also been authorised to put you on the payroll. You'll have to come down to the station and do some paperwork, then we can give you an hourly rate. It's not a fortune, before you get too excited.'

Dana was sure that whatever the pay rate was, it would seem like a fortune to her, having survived on ramen and tap water for so long while the store floundered along. So she was going to darn well be excited, whether Wade liked it or not. 'Sounds great!' she chirped. 'See you soon!'

One of the perks — in fact, the only perk — of owning a guitar store where hardly anything ever sold, was that Dana was feeling increasingly confident about leaving Brody in charge when she had to pop out. She knew that he could handle any guitar string sale enquiries. In fact, he would probably spend way too long on them, quizzing the prospective customer on the type of guitar they owned, the style of music they played, whether they played outdoors more often than indoors, and so on.

And if there was a bigger sale in the offing, or a more detailed query that only Dana could handle, he knew how to get hold of her. She held a tiny yet persistent hope that she'd return to the store to find that he'd made a four-figure sale. Hey, dreams are free.

Brody puffed his chest out when she told him he was in charge again. He flicked imaginary dust off the counter with his feather duster, and straightened some of the bags of guitar strings that Dana had just straightened a minute ago.

'Don't worry about the shop, boss,' he said. 'It's in safe hands with me.' He leaned forward onto the counter, accidentally hitting the No Sale button on the till, causing the cash drawer to spring out and slam into his chest. He staggered backwards and tripped over the stool behind him, and ended up sprawled on the ground.

'I'm not worried about the shop,' Dana muttered. 'It looks like it can defend itself.'

She raised her voice. 'Are you okay back there, Brodes?'

A wobbly thumbs-up emerged from behind the counter.

'All good, boss. Just a slippery patch of concrete there. I might as well dust some of the effect pedals on the bottom display shelf while I'm down here.'

Dana exhaled heavily. 'Just try to stay away from any of the expensive guitars, would you please?'

Shaking her head, she left the premises before she could change her mind about the whole thing.

***

Twenty minutes later, she had signed some papers at the station, and received a name tag in return. It wasn't quite the same as having a badge, but it did at least have the Police logo on it. Badly photocopied, but still.

Under her name, the badge read Consultant. Dana had never been a consultant before. It felt good. She was making her way up in the world. The last time she'd had something like that it was just a plastic lanyard that said 'Backstage Crew' from a local charity music festival. And she'd lost that lanyard when a disgruntled fan tore it off her after she stopped him from sneaking into the green room. Future archaeologists would probably find the plastic tag one day, amongst the stratified mud, beer cans and the odd stray shoe that was the hallmark of such events. Dana wondered if they would classify a find like that as a midden heap. They wouldn't be too far wrong.

'Ready?' Wade asked her.

She paused in the act of pinning on her new badge. 'Um. Ready? Are we starting now?'

Wade nodded. 'No time like the present. You've signed the papers. You're on police time now. We're off to the Stevens' house to establish a timeline.'

'Oh. Well then. Lead on, MacDuff,' she answered, straightening the name badge on her blouse.

Wade raised an eyebrow at her terminology, but waved her out through the reception area.

Lead on, MacDuff, she chastised herself. Where the hell did that come from?

Shaking her head, she moved on out towards the front door.

'Just give her a sec,' said Wade.

'Uh, give who a sec?'

'Mary.'

Dana gave him a blank look.

'Detective Mary Shaw, remember her?'

'Oh,' said Dana. 'Yes, of course. Is she joining us today?'

Wade looked amused. 'No,' he said, speaking slowly as though to a child. 'We're joining her. She's the detective, see? We're the extras in this situation.'

'Okay, gotcha,' said Dana as her cheeks heated up. 'But hey, I must be important too. I have a badge and everything.' She pointed to her name tag with mock pride.

Wade continued to do his best deadpan Jeeves impression, but she spotted a slight curl at the corners of his mouth as he rolled his eyes at her.

Detective Shaw burst out of a side room, in the middle of barking a stream of orders at various underlings who trailed in her wake.

Dana was impressed at how she commanded attention and respect. It couldn't be easy, in such a male-dominated work environment.

Shaw caught her looking, and gave her a quick nod. 'Thanks for coming in.' She immediately turned her attention to Wade. 'What are you standing there for? Go and bring the car around, please.'

'Yes, boss.' He disappeared out the door.

Once he'd gone, Shaw smiled at Dana. 'He's a

good officer, that one. Does what he's told.'

Dana got the message. She smiled back. 'You're obviously well-respected here.'

The detective inclined her head in acknowledgement, then checked her watch.

She caught Dana watching her. 'I know, I know, we've only been waiting two seconds. But I'm not timing Officer McNeish, I'm just thinking about all the other things I have to do today.'

'Oh, right,' said Dana, mentally adding this to her list of silver linings to owning a shop that wasn't very busy. Dana had very few tasks on her daily list, and all the time in the world to get them done. There were, of course, many downsides too, like not being able to afford dinner sometimes. So Dana was determined to prove her worth today, then maybe she'd get some more work with the police, and maybe a steadier cashflow.

Her overriding concern, of course, was to help the police find out who had killed Gene Stevens, and stolen his irreplaceable guitar. The money ran a distant second to that.

CHAPTER 7

Dana had never been in a police car before, and the ten-year-old kid in her was delighted. She found herself grinning from ear to ear, and almost hoping they spotted a miscreant in the act of doing miscreational stuff, so they could use the siren and lights.

Lost in a justice-dispensing daydream, she jumped when Detective Shaw addressed her.

'You okay back there, love?'

'Yes, fine thanks,' Dana replied.

'Right-o.' Shaw cleared her throat. 'Now, when we get there, I don't want you to say anything, are we clear? Not a word. You just stick near me, and try to look official. Yes?'

'Um, yes,' said Dana, trying out what she hoped was an official don't-mess-with-me face.

Shaw passed some documents back to her, and Dana shuffled through them. There was a crime scene photo (the one that technically shouldn't have been published in the news article), and what looked like transcripts of preliminary interviews with Maya and Devon Stevens. Suddenly, Dana's delight at being in a police car came to a crashing halt, as she was reminded of the seriousness of the situation. She shoved the documents into her handbag.

A few minutes later they pulled up at the Stevens house.

Dana gaped. Of course, she had known that Gene had practiced law, and had therefore probably been well off. She also knew he had owned a very expensive guitar. But somehow, even given that information, she had failed to put two and two together to realise that Gene had been properly wealthy.

Confronted by his palatial residence, the point was now painfully obvious.

The first clues were provided from the road, before you even pulled into the driveway. An ostentatious drystone wall separated the grounds – yes, there were actually grounds – from the outside world. Wrought iron gates fitted with security cameras and a buzzer provided another layer of protection from the hoi polloi.

Wade showed his badge to the camera, the gates swung open, and Dana got her first view of the parklike expanse within.

After what seemed like a very long time tootling along a sinuous tree-lined driveway, Dana was beginning to think they'd been transported to rural England somehow.

When the house finally hove into view, that impression was only reinforced.

Dana knew a lot about guitars and cats, but almost nothing about architecture. So when she described it to Brody later, all she could really say was that the house was large, pointy in some of the higher places, and it looked like the kind of residence that came with servants.

Shaw turned in her seat again. 'Remember what I said, please, Miss Osborne. No talking, even if spoken to.'

Dana nodded numbly, her jaw gaping at the opulence. She doubted she'd be able to speak even if she wanted to. It was all rather intimidating.

Wade took the lead at the front door, but he didn't even get a chance to knock. The door opened just as he reached up his hand. Surprise, surprise, there stood the butler.

'Hello, officers,' he said. 'My nephew is waiting for you in the library.'

Alright, then, Dana corrected herself. Not a

butler. Just an uncle who likes to dress formally. He had on an honest-to-goodness three-piece suit, in dark blue, with a salmon pink tie. As someone whose clothing choices tended towards the comfortable rather than the conspicuous, Dana was experiencing culture shock just looking at him.

The uncle waved them into a grand hallway, and they dutifully followed him through the house, like ducklings following mama duck on an educational waddle.

'Does he live here too?' Dana whispered to Shaw.

'No,' muttered Shaw. 'Just came along to support the family after what happened. He lives a few hours away, on a farm.'

'Aha. So, not a suspect, then?'

Shaw gave her a tight smile. 'You're catching on, rookie.'

They continued their manor house ramble in silence.

Detective Shaw strolled along with authority, looking around, and no doubt cataloguing the layout as she went.

Dana shuffled along in the rear, with her head swivelling around like a bobble-head doll.

It wasn't so much that there were numerous treasures to gaze at. It was just that everything was big. And tidy. And presumably expensive. The hallway was as wide as her living room, and the ceiling was so high it seemed to disappear behind clouds.

Dana honestly felt ambivalent about the whole place. On the one hand, it was opulent. On the other, she couldn't imagine living somewhere so… what was the word? So not-cosy.

If she lived somewhere like this, Paws McCartney would probably end up getting lost in the stables or whatever.

Oh wow, thought Dana. I bet they actually do have stables here. And a fellow who pops around on Sundays to polish the Rolls.

The hallway took them all the way through the centre of the house, and just before it opened out onto a pool area via ornate French doors, the uncle took a right turn and knocked on a dark wood-panelled door.

'Devon, they're here,' said the uncle.

There was no response from inside the library, but the uncle opened the door anyway and ushered them in.

'Just, if you don't mind, please take it easy on him,' he said as they went in. 'He's had a very trying time.'

'We understand,' said Shaw, offering up a police-issue Comforting Smile™. 'We're trained for this kind of thing.'

'Maybe I should come in too?' said the uncle.

Shaw turned, subtly blocking the entrance. 'We'd prefer to speak with Devon alone, at this time, if that's alright with you, sir?'

The uncle hesitated for a bit, then nodded. 'Of course, of course. No problem at all. I'll be in the kitchen if you need me. Second door on the left.'

'Thank you, sir.' said Shaw. 'Oh, by the way. Is Mrs Stevens in today?'

'Ah, well, yes, she is, but...' he fidgeted with his tie. 'You see, she's recuperating at the moment.'

Shaw nodded. Wade withdrew a notebook from one of his many pockets.

This action was not lost on the uncle.

He lowered his voice, and his eyes darted left and right as if checking for spies before he went on. 'I gave her a couple of sleeping pills to calm her nerves, you understand. She'll be out for a while.'

Dana wondered why this was being treated as such sensitive information. Having a reputation to uphold in the community must be tiring, she reflected.

The uncle scurried off, leaving them to trek across an expanse of polished wooden flooring, aiming for the silhouette of a young man standing by the windows at the far end of the room.

Shaw gestured to Wade, and he called out to Devon.

'Hello, it's Constable Wade McNeish, and I'm here with Detective Mary Shaw and our consultant Dana Osborne.'

Devon continued to stare out the window as if he was trapped in a Brontë novel. Dana's heart went out to him. It must be horrible to have your father murdered in your own home, and then to have to endure more questions from the police too.

Dana was glad she was merely a consultant, and didn't have to do any of the talking. She had no words for this.

Wade glanced at Shaw, and she gave a tiny nod. He approached Devon while the others kept their distance.

Dana couldn't hear what Wade was saying to Devon, but his voice was steady, calming and reassuring, as if he was tentatively approaching a horse of known skittishness. Eventually Devon seemed to focus on the room and realise there was company. He made apologetic noises, and Wade made consolatory ones back, all the while guiding the fellow over to a chair.

There was a semicircle of floomphy chairs near a dark wooden coffee table. Dana would have guessed the table was oak, but only because she thought that's what expensive desks were made of. If it wasn't a wood that was commonly used in guitar-making, she had no chance of identifying it.

Everybody took a seat, and that's when Dana discovered that the chairs which had seemed so floomphy were actually overstuffed bunions in disguise. Imagine being so wealthy that your furniture was uncomfortable!

Detective Shaw began.

'Devon, thank you so much for seeing us again at this time. We really appreciate it, and hope you understand we're only here to make sure we get all the information we need to speedily apprehend the person or persons responsible for your father's murder.'

Devon nodded distractedly. 'Yeah, I get it. You gotta do what you gotta do. I hope I can help.'

'Right then. Firstly, could you just please tell us again your movements on the night in question?'

Dana tried not to fidget uncomfortably. This was such an awkward situation, to be an observer of someone's grief, while another person was making them relive it.

Devon cleared his throat. 'Sure. Well, as I said last time, I was out in the stables, working on my car late that night.'

Are you kidding me? thought Dana. *They actually do have stables here!*

She nodded knowingly, as though all her friends had houses with stables, and uncles who looked like butlers, and capacious wood-panelled libraries.

Shaw pressed on. 'And where was your father while you were working on the car?'

'He was giving lessons in his studio.'

'Which is located where?'

Devon waved a hand towards the other side of the house. 'It's a room that comes off the kitchen, over that way.'

Shaw looked out through the library windows to the back garden area, which was a football field's worth of landscaped perfection. Dana followed her gaze, and noticed the building that must be the stables, set off to one side.

'Is the studio visible from the stables?' Shaw asked.

Devon shrugged. 'Yeah, if you're standing at the door. But I wasn't. I was inside, working on my car.'

Shaw nodded. 'Right. So you worked on the car, and then..?'

'I came back to the main house,' said Devon, 'at about, oh, two in the morning, and I noticed the back door was open, which is unusual, and… and that's when…' he took a shuddering breath. 'That's when I discovered Dad.'

Shaw nodded, and Wade was writing everything down. Dana just tried to look professional and supportive at the same time.

She was so busy trying to emote that she almost missed it when Shaw clicked her fingers at her and mouthed: the documents.

Oh! Dana fished the police report out of her bag and handed it over. Shaw selected a photo and laid it on the table in front of Devon.

'This is the scene, as you found it, is that correct?'

Devon looked at the photo, and gave a small sound of distress. He nodded. 'Yes, that's right.'

'Devon,' said Shaw, 'I'm sorry but I need you to look closely at that photo and make extra sure that that's exactly how you found the room. Your father in that exact position, the drawers in his desk pulled out like that,' she paused for a second. 'Your father's guitar on the floor just there.' Shaw was watching Devon like a hawk, Dana noted.

Devon picked up the photo and went over it again. Dana was watching him too, now.

'Um, yeah,' said Devon eventually. 'That's exactly how I found... everything. When I came in.'

'Thank you, Devon,' said Shaw. 'Just one more question. The guitar in the picture belongs to your father, is that right?'

'I already went over this,' huffed Devon. 'How many times do I have to tell you? My father was killed with his own guitar. Are you happy? Do you need me to say it again? It was a 1961 Draydon Weka. I went with him when he took it to shows, I watched him play it in bands, from when I was kid. Hell, I can still quote you the serial number, he banged on about it so often. That was his idea of a bedtime story, talking about that axe and how much he loved it. And yes, he actually called it his axe, like he was featuring in a VHS tape of an Eighties hair-metal video or something. So for the last time, let me be clear. Someone used my dad's own guitar to kill him. Okay?'

'I'm sorry, Devon, I have to ask these questions,' said Shaw.

'What is it?' The words were out of Dana's lips before she realised she'd spoken.

'What is what?' said Devon.

'Miss Osborne,' said Shaw, glaring at her with the force of a thousand suns.

'The serial number,' said Dana. 'You said you knew it by heart. I just wondered what it is.'

Shaw's face was starting to go a deep, violent red.

'Oh,' said Devon. He thought for a second, and then recited a string of numbers. They sounded right for a guitar of that age. Which would be easily verified or disproved as soon as Dana checked her guitar databases back at work.

However, that wasn't the point.

'That's not the serial number on the guitar in the photo,' said Dana.

Devon paled. Wade shifted uncomfortably in his seat and tried not to look at Shaw, who was almost levitating at this point – hands clenched, teeth grinding.

'What the…?' said Devon. 'Really? Let me look at the photo again.' He snatched it up off the table and brought it up to his face for close scrutiny. After a minute he let out a deep breath. 'Shit, maybe that isn't Dad's guitar. But if that's true, then… what, you think someone stole it?' He held up the photo and tapped it with a finger. 'Swapped it for one that looks the same?'

'We don't know for sure,' said Shaw. 'That's why we've brought in a consultant.' She glared daggers at Dana. 'A silent partner to help us determine what has happened.'

Devon stood up and began to pace. 'This helps, right?' he said. 'This makes it easier for you to find the killer, right? You just need to find the guitar.'

Shaw brought up her hands. 'Yes, but it's probably not going to be that easy. In fact, finding stolen goods is often more difficult than finding a killer. But it will certainly help focus our investigation. Now, perhaps you could have a seat, and then tell us who else was in the house that night.'

Devon sat down, but his right leg jiggled as if waiting to be set free again. 'Just me and mum.'

'And your father's guitar students.'

'Of course, the students, yeah. But like I said, I didn't see them.'

'Perhaps your father had a list, or a timetable of some kind?'

'Yes I'm sure he'd have had something like that. Probably just names on a calendar.' Devon gave a sad smile. 'He was a pretty old school, analogue kind of guy. Didn't like using a computer if he didn't have to.'

Shaw rose from her seat. 'If you could get that information to us, it would be much appreciated. Thank you so much for your help. We'll see ourselves out.'

She made a curt motion to Dana and Wade, and they trooped out in silence.

CHAPTER 8

Once they were back in the car and heading down the driveway, Shaw made a prolonged hissing sound, like a tea kettle on the boil. Dana realised it was Shaw letting out the furious pressure she'd been holding in.

'Do you remember,' Shaw seethed, 'when I mentioned that you were not to speak at all during the interview?'

Dana gulped. 'Yes, but —'

'So what the hell was that all about?'

'It was just a way of checking.'

'Checking what, exactly? That he'd identified everything in the photo correctly?' Shaw loomed at Dana over the car's centre console. 'Like I'd already asked him to?'

Dana's heartbeat increased tempo dramatically. She felt like a field mouse in front of Shaw's eagle eyes.

'Well, yes, but he said it was his father's guitar,

and we know it isn't.'

Wade made a low whistle.

'So, you're saying Devon killed his own father?' said Shaw.

'Wait, no! I didn't say that!'

'You're the one who just accused him of lying to the police.'

'About the guitar, sure!' Dana threw up her hands. 'I think he's hiding something, but I never said I thought he'd killed Gene.'

Shaw huffed and turned back to the front windscreen. 'Well, good. He's got absolutely no motive as far as we can tell. There's no point in him stealing a guitar that would probably be his inheritance anyway.'

'It's just odd, that's all,' said Dana's mouth, much to the dismay of her brain, which was trying to shut the conversation down before Dana annoyed Shaw any more.

'What's odd?' Shaw barked.

'Well, only a person who's spent a lot of time with an instrument will know the serial number off by heart,' she said. 'If he knew the serial, there's no way he would mis-identify the fake.'

'Or,' Shaw declaimed, 'he could simply be suffering so much from his father's violent murder, that he's not thinking clearly.'

Dana shook her head. 'Devon's been attending guitar shows with his Dad since he was knee-high to a Telecaster. Guitar nerds like him don't make mistakes with serial numbers.'

'Even in times of great stress?'

'Especially in times of great stress. Gives them something to hold onto.'

'You'd know this, would you?'

Dana's heart clenched. Oh yes, she knew this alright. Knew it all too well. Flashes of memories assaulted her. The hallway outside Ziggy's motel room. The astringent smell of industrial cleaning products. The knowledge that she would soon be asked to identify her brother's body. The salt in the wound of being told that his guitar had been stolen by his killer. The excessively detailed report she was able to give the police about the guitar, from its serial number, down to the gouges on the back of the body, from Ziggy's Ostentatious Belt-Buckle phase.

Focusing on all those little details about Ziggy's guitar had been her way of clinging to her sanity as she processed her grief.

So, yes. She knew. Even if Devon was half-mad with grief right now, from what he'd told them about his history with his father's guitar, he'd surely have noticed it had been swapped with a fake.

Dana swallowed her own older but somehow still fresh grief, and simply said: 'Yes. I would.'

Shaw turned around to observe Dana for a minute, then eventually gave her a slow, knowing nod. 'Hmmm,' was all she said, as she settled back into her seat.

Dana tried to change the subject. 'So, what happens now?'

'For now, we continue with interviewing everyone who was anywhere near the house on the day.'

'Are there many people?'

Shaw nodded. 'As Devon said, his father had guitar students. There were about half a dozen over the course of the evening.'

Dana whistled.

'Is that a lot?' Shaw asked.

'It would be for me,' Dana admitted. 'I mean, wow, the guy must have been raking in the money at that rate.'

'Might explain the size of the castle we just visited,' said Shaw. She lifted a hand and directed Wade toward a drive-thru. 'Now, if you two don't mind, I'm going to get something to eat and then head back to the station for a wee bout of soul-crushing paperwork.'

CHAPTER 9

Wade drove them back to the station, with Shaw chomping happily on a burger. Dana was waiting to get home and make a sandwich. Until her first lot of police consultant money came through, there'd be no random takeaways for her. (Random Takeaways - good name for a song. Or a band. She filed it away in her ever-growing mental list.)

Dana wondered if Wade was in the same boat, financially, or if he just didn't eat that kind of thing. Hey, maybe he was vegetarian too, and she'd have someone to swap recipes with. Rockingham West wasn't exactly overrun with fields of self-sown vegetarians, so Dana often felt like the odd one out in social grazing scenarios.

Either way, it gave her a chance to ask him a question that had been percolating at the back of her mind for a few minutes now. Her thoughts were circling around the palatial residence that Gene had called home.

'Wade,' she said. 'The house had security cameras, right? Didn't they catch anything? Like, a person leaving with a guitar, for example?'

'There was a whole lot of that,' Wade replied, navigating a roundabout as they edged back into the less desirable part of town. 'People leaving with guitars, that is. In fact, there was too much of that, with all Gene's students who were booked that night. We've got hours of footage of people coming and going with guitar cases, so any one of them could have been the thief, the killer, or both.'

'Nobody else?' said Dana. 'Someone who wasn't a student?'

'We've got someone back at the station scrubbing through all the footage now, so if there is anyone else, we'll know soon.'

'Hmmm,' said Dana. 'You have an actual person doing that? I thought it would all be artificial intelligence by now. Like Gibson's self-tuning guitars.'

'Hah!' Wade laughed. 'Think about how much money a company like Gibson makes compared to how much the police make. The moment AI becomes cheaper than hiring a first-year police cadet, that's when the future will arrive in the force.'

'Fair point.'

Wade glanced at Dana in the rear view mirror. 'Can I drop you back at your shop? It's on our way.'

Shaw snorted with a mouthful of burger.

'Well, it's almost on our way,' Wade amended.

'That would be great,' said Dana. 'Saves me a bit of a trek.'

'No problem.'

A few minutes later she was at the door of the Pick Me Guitar Shop. As she got out of the car she noticed Wade and Shaw giving the place the once-over.

It was hard not to notice that Brody was stuck to the front window, blatantly staring at Dana and her ride. He wore an excited grin, and appeared to be bouncing up and down. This was a little unsettling, but since the place hadn't burned down, Dana was feeling mildly hopeful that leaving him in charge for a few hours hadn't been a catastrophic decision which she would regret till the end of time.

Shaw popped her head out the car window. 'Are you free tomorrow afternoon?' she called out.

'Absolutely. What are you thinking?'

'We'll get the guitar students' names from Devon and start interviewing them,' said Shaw. 'Same deal as today. You're along to spot anything weird that's guitar-related. And you're not to -'

'- speak unless you ask me to,' Dana finished for her. 'Got it. I won't do it again. I'm fully onboard and will comply with all directives.' She gave Shaw a salute.

Shaw fixed her with a baleful glare. And continued to do so as the car drove off. She kept eye contact until the car rounded a corner and was lost behind a building.

'I think she's warming to me,' Dana said to herself, with a wee smile.

She turned and strode into the store, and was immediately pounced on, first by Paws McCartney, then Brody.

As she detached Paws McCartney's claws from her leg – a delicate yet painful operation accompanied by many a muffled curse – she tried to make sense of the stream of words pouring out of Brody's mouth. He was speaking so fast he couldn't even form coherent sentences. Spittle flew from the corners of his mouth, and his eyes were saucers.

If she didn't know him any better, she'd say he was on drugs, for sure. But one of the reasons she kept him on at the shop was because he never touched the naughty stuff. Okay, one time she'd caught him smoking some kind of sweet herb out the back during his break, but she'd put her foot down and he knew to not do that during working hours now.

He'd been a model employee since then. Well, in terms of attendance anyway. He got a gold star for turning up each day. She'd have liked it if he also had some kind of sales technique too, but, to paraphrase a wise old rocker: getting what you want isn't always a feasible option.

She wasn't convinced that Brody was what she needed either, but he was certainly… present.

Unfortunately, his manic performance had scared Paws, and now Dana bore the scars.

'Could you calm down a bit, Brody, please?' she pleaded. Maybe she should let him have a smoke just this once. It might round the edges off him.

'Sorry sorry sorry!' said Brody. ' Yeah, okay, yeah, it's just that there's news.' He grabbed her arms. 'There's news, Dana!'

Dana shrugged off Brody's hands and then removed Paws' last claw. The mercurial cat sped off into the back room, no doubt headed for the comfort of the office chair that he'd permanently claimed.

'News,' said Dana. 'My, that does sound exciting. How about we sit down quietly and you tell me about it from the start, in a slow voice, and remembering to breathe? Can you breathe for me please, Brody?'

She guided him through a few deep breaths in and out, until his dilated pupils began to return to normal.

'Can I get you a cup of tea?' she asked.

'No time for tea,' said Brody. 'I have news!'

'Okay, what is this news then?'

'Ziggy's guitar has been sold.'

Dana's heart forgot how to do hearty stuff for a while. Then her lungs joined in the general strike. She just stood there while her mouth opened and closed. Central processing error, core shutdown imminent.

Brody continued to gabble at her, but she needed air. She needed to sit down. She definitely could do with a strong cup of tea or two.

She brushed past Brody and staggered up to her flat.

'Wait!' Brody called out. 'Don't you want to hear about this?'

'In a minute!' She managed to force the words out, thankful that the movement of her legs was causing her internal organs to resume normal service.

'Give me a sec while I put the jug on. Close the shop and come up and tell me everything.'

'Close the shop?' said Brody, hovering at the bottom of the stairs that led up to her flat. 'What about the customers?'

'I don't think we need to worry too much about that, do you?'

Brody thought about it for a second. 'I guess not, really.'

A few minutes later, Dana was sitting on her couch with a fresh cup of tea as Brody barrelled into the dining room/lounge/kitchen of her small flat.

'News!' he said, although he was still quite excited so it was more like a shout.

'Sit,' said Dana, pointing at a chair. 'Calm down. Speak softly. Start from the beginning.' She was hoping that if she treated him like a puppy she'd be able to train him to behave.

It had a limited effect. At least he stopped shouting.

'I was checking out a guitar forum - '

'While working in the shop?' Dana interjected.

Brody put his hands up. 'While working in the shop. In between serving customers, and cleaning guitars, I checked out a guitar forum.'

Dana sighed. 'Did you sell anything today, by the way?'

'Ahhhh,' Brody had to think about that. 'Yeah. Actually, I did sell a few packs of strings, and two ukuleles.' He beamed.

Dana did the sums in her head. That was enough to cover Brody's wages, pretty much. So, not a total loss.

'Anyway,' Brody continued. 'This forum had a post from Mikey Thunderbird, so everyone was going a bit wild, because when he posts on there you know it's going to be something big.'

Dana sipped her tea, and nodded. Mikey Thunderbird was a child guitar prodigy, or rather he had been, but now he was all grown up. So, now he was simply a good guitar player, Dana supposed. Time could be cruel.

Anyway, Dana was aware that, as Mikey's star rose, he'd begun collecting rare and high-end guitars, and these days he was rumoured to have one of the largest collections in the world. Not just of guitars, but amplifiers, old advertising posters, the works. Mikey was the guitar obsessive's guitar obsessive. One of the very few people whose income and connections had grown at the same rate as his burning need to collect everything.

Some people thought him a show-off, flaunting his wealth like that. But anyone who'd actually met him said that he was a genuine guitar fan, and did it all for the love of the instrument. To preserve its history, not for bragging rights.

To other guitar fans, he was generous with his

time and knowledge. Rare guitar dealers loved him, not just because he was a good customer, but also because of the genuine delight on his face whenever he scored something he'd been searching for.

Dana wished she could get hold of the kind of guitars that would interest Mikey. She'd quite happily feed that obsession.

'He had this countdown going,' Brody was saying. 'Like: in ten minutes I'm gonna show you all something that I've just bought that's gonna blow your mind. So I stayed online - '

'While keeping an eye out for customers looking to buy a guitar,' Dana put in.

'- while keeping an eye out for customers looking to buy a guitar, for sure. I would definitely have spotted one of those.' Brody shook his head. 'But no luck. Anyway, ten minutes later, Mikey teases us with a photo. It's the headstock of an old Strat.'

Dana's heart flipped again. 'Front or back of the headstock?'

'Front.'

'No serial number, then?'

'Not yet,' said Brody, his left leg starting to jiggle up and down. 'But more photos keep coming. The next one is the tone control and input jack.'

'Let me guess,' said Dana. 'The tone control is actually from a Mustang, like a Jazz Bass style one, not from a Strat.' It wasn't even a question. If it was Ziggy's guitar, that's how it would be.

Dana could remember her brother grabbing that tone control – off her own Mustang! – one morning, after he'd lost his one at a gig the night before. Sometimes his performance theatrics took a heavy toll on his gear. 'I need it more than you, sis,' he'd told her. Since she was still just learning to play at this stage, and her older brother was already starting to get good support gigs, she'd let him have it. It actually gave her a thrill to see something of hers up onstage with him. Made her feel connected. Made her feel part of something exciting. She still had that Mustang. And it still didn't have a tone knob. And it never would.

'That's right!' cried Brody, jolting her out of her reverie. 'And more photos came. And all the details were right, Dana, just like you've always said. Eventually there's a photo of the whole guitar, and Mikey Thunderbird's holding it, and he's standing in Zander's Rare Guitars, in the VIP back room. And he says he's just bought the guitar of the greatest guitar player who ever lived.'

Dana swallowed. 'But who'd he buy it from?'

'They wouldn't say. Like, you know, Zander is the middle guy - '

'Intermediary.'

'Yeah, the middle guy. He sets these things up but he never says who the seller is.'

Dana set her mug down.

'I need to find that seller.'

Brody's leg stopped jiggling. 'Why? What are you going to do?'

'Whoever sold that guitar might be the last person to ever see my brother alive. I need to know what happened.'

Brody sat in silence with her for a minute, which was both a nice change and a blessed relief. He knew the depth of feeling that Dana had about her brother's demise, and he simply didn't have the words to plumb them. But he could sit there and support her with his presence. For a certain amount of time anyway.

About thirty seconds, in this case.

'Ahem. Maybe I should go and open up again?' he said, standing up and brushing imaginary lint off his jeans. Dana nodded, and he toddled off down the stairs.

A few seconds later Dana heard the slap of the Closed sign transitioning to Open, and the bell above the door tinkled in misguided anticipation.

Dana went and refilled her cup of tea, then settled into the sofa again. It had been a long day. A busy day. An interesting day. Too interesting, really.

Murders, musicians and Mustang tone knobs.

She raised her cup to the ghost of Ziggy. 'I'll find out what happened to you,' she promised. 'And if I can, I'll get your guitar back too.'

The next day, Dana fired up her tired old steam-powered laptop, made a cup of tea while it built up the requisite pressure, then sent an email to Zander's Rare Guitars.

Zander, of the eponymous guitar shop, was an enigma. Simultaneously a smiling, charming, people person; and also a complete shadow. He was known only as Zander. Was it his first name or surname? Was it fabricated or was he born with it? Nobody knew.

But if you asked anyone in the guitar world – Aotearoa region – to name the best rare guitar dealer in the business, the answer was always that one name: Zander.

Dana was one of the very few people who had actually broached his perimeter, then explored, surveyed and mapped some of his personal territory. Initially, she had bumped into him at trade shows, and even though they were in completely different leagues, business-wise, they'd bonded over a love of guitars and the idea that the right instrument could put a player in touch with the foundational vibrations of the universe, when used correctly.

A few jam sessions had resulted, but they'd never gone so far as to make up an actual band, and play an actual venue. There'd been one night when the jam went through to the wee small hours, and Zander had crashed on Dana's couch, when she thought he might have been interested in her for more than her chord inversions, as the saying goes. But Dana wasn't interested in beginning a relationship - with anyone, really. It's just the way she was wired. She liked hanging out with cool people sometimes, and liked being on her own the rest of the time. So, they hadn't gotten together for a little while now, because even though she enjoyed his company, it felt a little awkward after that. Nonetheless, she thought they were still good enough friends that Zander would take her request seriously.

Sure enough, a few minutes later, just enough time for Paws McCartney to jump off the cash register and install himself on Dana's laptop like some kind of furry malware, a reply from Zander pinged into her inbox.

Ah, those ten words we all know and love: you've got mail, pertaining to your dead brother's stolen guitar.

Is not exactly what her computer said, but that was the vibe.

Zander's message was brief, which was lucky because Dana could only just read it over the top of Paws' fuzzy bulk: 'I'm free now if you want to come and talk about this ZZZZZZZZZZZZ'. That last part was courtesy of Paws. Dana closed the mail app before Paws could send Zander a puzzling mono-runic reply.

Leaving her helpful feline to keep the laptop warm, Dana went to tell Brody he was now in charge of the shop for the whole day.

'No problem, boss!' He said brightly. 'Wow, it's like I'm the store manager these days, huh?'

'That's right,' said Dana, patting his shoulder. 'And if you can sell more guitars, I'll be able to pay you a bit more to go with that promotion.'

She left Brody with a thoughtful expression on his face, no doubt pondering various harebrained schemes to sell more instruments.

***

At Zander's Rare Guitars, she was welcomed at

the door by the man himself, and he looked very apologetic.

'I thought it wouldn't be long till I heard from you,' said Zander, as he enveloped her in a hug. 'I'm so sorry I couldn't tell you ahead of time, but Mikey T wanted it kept secret, and the seller didn't want their name mentioned anywhere, so it was all a bit hush-hush, you know?'

Dana did not know, actually. She could only imagine what it must be like to deal with the rich, the famous, and the obsessive collectors. Frankly, she found that all the drama around the sale of iconic guitars could sometimes descend into the distasteful, and was rather pleased that her customers were just normal people who appreciated a guitar for what it was rather than who had once owned it.

One time, a well-to-do gentleman had come into her store, and loudly proclaimed he was there to buy the best guitar in the place. Instead, he ended up walking out with the most expensive one. To a guitar nerd like Dana, that was not the same thing. But, he was happy with the purchase, and Dana had shown him a range of quality instruments, and was happy to sell him that one.

Still, she had to admit that it would be nice to have Ziggy's old guitar in her possession, due to all the memories it represented. Oh hell, had she become one of those obsessed collectors? Isn't that all they wanted, after all? An instrument that was associated with someone they looked up to. Does it make any difference if it's family?

Anyway, putting all that aside, the number one thing she needed today was the name of the seller, so she could track back to whoever might know what had happened in Ziggy's motel room all those years ago. Getting hold of the guitar itself would merely be a nice bonus, although extremely unlikely.

Zander released her, and she smiled at him. 'It's nice to see you again. It's been a while.'

'I know, right?' he agreed. 'When was the last time we caught up? Probably that school charity thing, yeah?'

'Oh, yeah,' said Dana. 'That's right. I wish I hadn't been a judge for the talent quest that day. It disqualified me from entering the draw to win that guitar you donated.'

Zander laughed. 'Like you don't have enough guitars to choose from already?'

Dana raised an eyebrow. 'Look who's talking, mister "I collect any guitar from 1963".'

'Ahhhh,' Zander took a deep breath and slowly let it out. 'There's something about that year, Dana.'

He shook his head wistfully. 'Guitars from that year… I don't know. They just have an aura of magic around them.'

Dana chuckled. 'Don't all guitars?'

'Huh,' said Zander, waving a finger from side to side. 'Not all of them, I don't think. Anyway, come into the office and we'll talk.'

They walked through the shop. First there was a huge front room filled with nice guitars, and then, from a corridor down the back, various smaller rooms branched off. Some were filled with nicer guitars, some with extremely nice guitars, heck there was even a room just for boutique strings and pickups.

Zander had his own pickup winding machine, staffed by a woman in her late eighties who used to work on the production line at a big-name guitar factory. Customers could book an appointment with her, discuss their requirements, and come out with a bespoke set of pickups tailored to their playing style.

This wasn't even the most impressive part of Zander's setup. No, you had to keep going down the corridor for that, and most people never got that far.

Only Zander had the key to the door at the end, and he only admitted certain people through that sacred portal, to the Vault.

The most recent visitor had, of course, been Mikey Thunderbird. And now it was Dana's turn.

Zander put the key in the lock, turned back to give Dana a smile that said 'wait till you get a load of this', and then swung the door open.

Some called it Zander's Grotto. Some called it the Rare Room. But everyone called it a thing of wonder.

Dana had heard the stories. She'd seen random parts of the room in the background of videos like the one with Mikey Thunderbird. Intellectually, she knew that Zander had been trading in rare guitars for a long time. But actually seeing the Vault in person was close to a religious experience.

An imaginary choir sang in her head as she surveyed the room. It wasn't a huge space, but every square centimetre was crammed with guitar-y gems. They filled every spot on the walls, they reclined on stands on the floor, and a select few hung resplendent inside locked display cases.

Every single one of them was probably worth more on its own than the entire stock in Dana's shop.

Zander strode to the centre of the room and beamed at Dana. 'Welcome to the Vault,' he said, and spun on his heel with his arms out wide. 'You can try some of these out if you like.'

Dana realised this was the most Willy Wonka moment she would probably ever encounter. With some effort, she managed to stop gawping at guitars for a second, and reeled her jaw back in from where it had dropped. 'Thanks, but I really just want to talk about Ziggy's guitar if that's okay?'

Zander looked a teensy bit disappointed. 'Sure. Fair enough. Take a seat, please.'

He motioned her towards a comfy-looking couch.

'I knew you'd want more details,' he said as they settled in. 'So I quizzed the seller pretty hard. Oh, let me just say first of all, that Mikey Thunderbird would like to invite you to his house to look at the guitar, and chat about it. You know he's a huge guitar nut, and he loves to have all the provenance, and any stories attached to the instrument.'

'Well, sure,' Dana replied. 'I guess that's what I'm looking for too, really. Just gotta fill in the gaps between now and back when…' she choked up for a second. '…you know, the last time I saw it.'

Zander nodded sympathetically. 'Okay. The seller, who wishes to remain anonymous…' Dana gritted her teeth at that, but held her tongue. She would have liked to speak to the seller in person, but if Zander had all the details she needed to hear, then it wouldn't matter.

Zander continued. 'They said they bought the guitar about a month after Ziggy passed away.'

Dana tried to control her breathing. Dammit, a one month long missing link between the previous owner and the last time Ziggy was seen alive. And this was three years ago, so how was she going to figure out who had it in between those times?

'Now, don't worry,' said Zander. 'I told you I grilled 'em good, didn't I?' He smiled. 'The seller said they got the guitar from a roadie that was working on Ziggy's tour.'

Dana's heart lurched. 'His guitar tech? No way. I know Eli and he would never have taken Zig's guitar, let alone sold it.'

'The seller didn't say guitar tech, they only said roadie,' Zander clarified. 'There might have been, what? A dozen roadies on the crew, for a tour that size?'

'Oh,' said Dana. 'Right. Um, I think there were eight of them, between the drum tech, bass guy, Eli, plus lighting and sound.'

'Okay then. So the seller didn't say which one it was, but I hope that's helped you narrow down your search a bit?'

'Absolutely,' said Dana. 'Thank you so much, Zander.'

She was grateful to Zander for the special effort

he'd made on her behalf, but was having trouble showing it, because of the freshly revived grief she was feeling over her brother. Was it really possible that one of his roadies — a member of supposedly tight-knit crew who ate, slept and breathed together while on tour — could have taken Ziggy's guitar as he lay dead in a motel room? Surely there was another explanation for this. Well, she was just going to have to keep digging to find out. At least, like Zander said, she now had a shortlist of people to talk to about it.

She plastered a smile on her face and thanked Zander again.

'I really appreciate you doing that for me, Zander.' She got up to leave. 'I have to head off now, but please feel free to pass my contact details on to Mikey Thunderbird. I'd be happy to meet with him and talk about the guitar.'

As they walked to the door, a thought struck her.

'Hey, while I'm here,' she said. 'I'm helping the police with the investigation of Gene Stevens' murder. Just wondering if you've seen his old Draydon Weka around.'

'Oh, yeah, that was horrible news,' said Zander. 'But I thought they said the killer used his own Weka to do it? Don't they have it at the police station now?'

'Turns out it was a copy, not his actual guitar. So now we're trying to find out where it ended up.'

Zander's face went pale. The thought of an original '61 Weka going missing was terrifying to a rare guitar connoisseur like him.

'Shit. So he was killed with a Bluff? A fake Weka?' He thought about it for a minute, then shook his head. 'If someone took the real one, it will have gone underground, I reckon. Probably never see it again now, unless the thief dies, or someone else nicks it from them.' He tilted his head. 'Or… maybe the thief doesn't know the true worth of what they've stolen. In that case, there's a chance someone has seen it around.' He perked up at that idea. 'I'll put out feelers and let you know if I turn anything up, okay?'

'That would be great. Thanks again, Zander.'

'Don't mention it, Dana. What goes around, comes around. We're all just strings on the same guitar, I reckon.'

Dana just had time to get back to her shop and check in with Brody before her afternoon consultancy gig with the police began.

Brody had not only sold three sets of strings, but also an honest-to-goodness actual guitar - a student model that was bundled with a practice amp.

Dana was impressed. And relieved. Between her sideline work for the police, and Brody's burgeoning sales skills, it was beginning to look like the best week they'd had in a while, fiscally speaking. Paws McCartney would be dining on his favourite cat food tonight.

She smiled, realising this is what getting older feels like. When your idea of a good way to celebrate a windfall is to treat your cat to a nice dinner.

'Okay, Brodes,' she said, giving the smiling shop assistant a pat on the shoulder. 'While I'm out this afternoon, maybe see if you can break your new sales record, huh?'

'Will do, boss. I'm on a roll!' Brody was ecstatic. 'It's really picked up since I handed around some business cards at the gig the other night.'

Dana stopped mid-pat.

'Wait,' she said. 'You handed out business cards? That was a great idea.'

'Thanks' he beamed.

'But we don't have business cards.' Dana's brow furrowed. 'So what did you hand out?'

Brody tapped the side of his nose. 'That was the clever part.'

Uh oh, thought Dana. Here it comes.

'At the last trade show you took me to, I got some cards from each booth. Then I crossed out the name of their company and wrote in ours.'

'Oh, Brody, please tell me you're joking.'

Brody's smile disappeared. 'Um. Okay then,' he said in a small voice. 'I'm joking.'

As she often found herself doing when interacting with Brody, Dana sighed.

'What's the problem?' he said. 'I mean, they were giving the cards away. They never said you couldn't re-use them. And besides, they had pictures of cool guitars on them.' He shrugged. 'They were made for sharing! Collect the set, kind of thing.'

Dana was torn. Brody was sweet for trying out a

new idea, but he'd also potentially made her guitar shop's name mud with a whole lot of suppliers.

Then again, he had a point. If people came to her shop to buy guitars supplied by those suppliers, it was a win-win, wasn't it? She got a sale, they got a sale...

She guessed she would find out in due course.

Dana made herself a quick sandwich and filled up the catfood bowl, which Paws swiftly emptied.

'My goodness, Mr McCartney,' she said, scratching him behind the ears. 'You hoovered that up so quick I don't think it even had time to touch the bottom of the bowl.'

Paws didn't dignify that with a response. He simply hopped up on a kitchen chair, wiped his face once or twice, turned in a circle for a critically specific number of times, then promptly fell asleep.

That was his work done for the next few hours.

By the time Dana stepped out the front door of the shop, her ride was already there waiting, as if she was some kind of rock star. She fleetingly imagined what it must be like to be Bonnie Raitt, or St Vincent. Presumably it was all hot and cold running chauffeurs. Three different kinds of water to choose from in the green room. The massive weight of pressure to perform at one hundred and ten percent every night to thousands of critical fans… hmmmm, yeah. Maybe she was happy with her life after all.

Constable Wade McNeish was sitting at the wheel of the unmarked police car, stoic as ever, putting on his I'm professional and dependable face for Detective Shaw. The first time Dana met him, he'd been a lot more informal, but she guessed that informality was probably not the best way to impress your superiors in the police force.

Detective Shaw was poking through a small plastic container, with a look of disgust on her face.

'Hi,' said Dana, jumping into the back of the car. 'How are you two today? What's in the box, Detective? A piece of evidence?'

'Urgh, no,' replied Shaw. 'It's a piece of…salad.' She made the word sound like a tropical disease. 'My wife is trying to get me to eat this rubbish instead of actual food..'

'Oh,' said Dana. 'Your wife? I didn't realise…'

'What? That I was married?'

'Ah. Yes. Yeah, that's what I meant. Sorry, I didn't notice the ring till just now. Congrats!'

Dana felt the heat creeping into her face as she continued to dig herself a conversational hole to fall into. Stop talking, stop talking, change the subject!

'You're a bit late with the congratulations,' said Shaw. 'I've been married to Hinemoa for three years now, but thank you anyway.' She gazed mournfully at the salad, sighed, and closed the container. 'I'll need more than this to go on, if I'm gonna get through all these interviews today.' She looked at Wade. 'Let's hit Boss Burgers on the way, shall we?'

He nodded. 'Yes, ma'am.' Dana could see the corners of his mouth twitch up, and there was a twinkle in his eyes. He couldn't have looked any more keen for a burger unless he started salivating right there and then. Her dreams of having a fellow vegetarian to hang out with were, sadly, scythed like so much wheat.

Shaw turned in her seat to talk to Dana. 'It's an energy thing, you see. My blood sugar gets low. People don't understand. Now.' She pulled a sheet of paper from a file next to her feet, and handed it to Dana. 'Here's a list of the people we're seeing today. They were all students of Mr. Stevens.'

'And they all had lessons on the night of... on that night?' Dana was avoiding saying the word 'murder' if at all possible. To think that something so horrible could happen to someone she knew. It was distressing.

'That's right,' Shaw replied. 'Recognise any of the names?'

Dana skimmed the list. Yes, in fact, she did know a couple of people on the list, and one of them had been in her store very recently. Rawiri James, the late-night guitar string desperado.

He'd seemed like a nice guy. Dana was sure he couldn't be the killer. Not that you could really tell by how nicely someone asked for guitar strings.

Rawiri was second on the list of visits. A woman called Stephanie Ngata was first. After the burgers, of course.

Dana had the dubious pleasure of watching the two police officers make short work of some deep-fried comestibles, and then, a mere ten minutes later, they were at Stephanie Ngata's house. Wade knocked on the door. Detective Shaw stood at his shoulder. Dana stood several paces back. On the naughty step, as it were, after the telling-off from the last interview she took part in. Backing singers were called that for a reason, she reasoned. The limelight was not for her, but the ranking officer.

The door opened to reveal a young woman, about twenty years old, Dana guessed.

Even though the visit was scheduled, Stephanie still had that mildly terrified expression that most people tend to adopt when confronted with uniformed officers. Dana remembered being stopped in her car for a breath alcohol test once, and freaking out about it, even though she knew she hadn't touched a drop all evening. While she waited the ten or so seconds for the result, she managed to convince herself that it would somehow incorrectly return a positive, and she'd be taken to jail, and bad women would be mean to her. Subsequently, when the officer let her go with a cheery wave, she almost broke down and cried.

Reflecting on this, Dana decided that if she ever won the lottery, she'd treat herself to some really top-class therapy.

She startled back into the present moment when Stephanie invited them all in, offering them the obligatory cup of tea as they took a seat in the lounge.

Dana spotted a guitar leaning in a corner, near a tidy, classic-looking, small valve amplifier. The guitar was a Superstrat style, the kind of thing that was versatile enough to play any kind of music on. It was a nice combination - something Dana herself would choose.

Once everyone was settled in, the interview began.

After a bit of back and forth, with Wade taking the lead again while Shaw and Dana observed, it emerged that Stephanie hadn't seen anything out of the ordinary on the night in question. She'd been scheduled for the first lesson of the night, and Gene had seemed fine.

When Wade had been through his repertoire of interview questions, he asked Stephanie if he could look around her house.

'I'm sorry to have to do this, but it's just standard procedure. I hope that's okay?'

'Of course,' said Stephanie. 'And if you find my bus pass anywhere I'd be grateful to see it again.' She gave a nervous laugh.

Wade gave her a smile, then slipped from the room.

Now it was Shaw's turn to be quizmaster.

'Did you see Gene's son, Devon, that night?'

'Um, not really. I mean, I saw him on his way out to the shed at the back and that's it. What does he call it? The stables, I think.'

Dana noticed the rolling of the eyes which accompanied this piece of information.

Stephanie went on. 'I was kinda pleased that Devon didn't hang around, actually.'

'Why's that?'

'Oh, he was always trying to show off in front of his dad, if there was a student there. Like, he'd loudly sigh if you hit a bum note or whatever. He wasn't very encouraging of players who didn't come up to his standard. Gene would have to shoo him away sometimes.'

'I see. And Mrs Stevens?'

'Oh no, she's never around when lessons are on,' said Stephanie, with a wry smile. 'I get the impression she doesn't like guitars very much, from what Gene said.'

'What did he say, exactly?'

Stephanie thought for a second. 'I guess, things like, he was allowed to play with his guitars as long as he kept the lawyering money rolling into the joint bank account.'

'Right,' said Shaw with a small smile of her own. 'So, you had your lesson, and Mr Stevens was behaving exactly as normal?'

'Yeah. We've been working on my bends.'

Dana had the pleasure of seeing Shaw look scandalised.

'She means bending a guitar string to change the pitch of a note,' Dana whispered.

'Oh.'

'I have endless trouble,' Stephanie continued, 'because my guitar keeps going out of tune.'

'Oh, that should be an easy fix,' said Dana. 'On a guitar like yours, with a tremolo arm, it might just need a bit of adjusting, or else we can look at your machine heads. Worst case scenario, they'll need replacing, but that's not too expensive. But, believe it or not, most of the time it can be fixed by dragging a pencil over the nut slots. Graphite is a very good lubricant - stops the strings sticking.'

Wade had appeared at the doorway. He cleared his throat and Dana finally realised that Shaw was staring at her, mouth set in a line, with a vein pulsing in her forehead.

But before Shaw could berate her, Stephanie chirped up. 'Oh thanks! Can I drop my guitar in to your shop sometime so you can have a look?'

'Absolutely,' said Dana hurriedly, trying to reverse herself out of the car crash she'd created. 'Any time.'

***

The ride to the next interview was a quiet one. Not a restful kind of quiet. A tense kind of quiet; the kind where you could cut the air with a blunt butter knife.

Dana was hoping she hadn't done herself out of a job. She was still in the car, so that was a good sign.

Shaw's face had cooled from a furious purple to a slightly less angry red. Surely another good sign.

Wade was quiet, but looked amused by the situation. Dana thought that might be some kind of a good sign, but it could go either way.

Detective Shaw kept opening her mouth to say

something, then just giving up. Eventually she composed and delivered a full sentence.

'Miss Osborne, since you continue to believe it's your duty to lead this investigation, perhaps you have some thoughts on the interview that you'd like to share with us?'

Dana cleared her throat.

'Actually, yes, I do.'

'Oh, really? The floor is yours, milady,' said Shaw, with a sweeping gesture.

'Firstly, I just want to be extra clear that we're not considering Stephanie as a suspect, right?'

'Hmmm,' said Shaw. 'Technically, we have to treat everyone as a suspect, but...'

'Surely not!' Dana interjected. 'For one thing, I don't think Stephanie would have the upper body strength to use a heavy guitar to smash someone over the head. She's tiny, right?'

'I'll grant you that,' said Shaw.

'For another thing, her own guitar and amplifier were in immaculate condition. Better than showroom condition, even.'

'And this tells you what?'

'I just don't think someone who looks after their gear like that would defile an instrument by... by, you know...'

'By getting blood all over it?'

Dana swallowed. 'Yes, that.'

Shaw pondered this for a minute. 'Well,' she eventually pronounced, 'though none of that is definitive proof, I tend to agree with you. And let's not forget, she was the first student of the evening, so she would have had to come back after the others had gone, which increases her chances of being spotted lurking around the area. Given that, what else were you thinking?'

'Okay. This is just a gut feeling, now.'

'I'd expect nothing less,' said Shaw, which left Dana trying to decide whether to be flattered or offended.

'Right.' She soldiered on. 'Well, I got the feeling that Stephanie didn't think much of Maya and Devon, but only because she picked that vibe up off Gene.'

'How do you mean?'

'It seems to me that Stephanie was reflecting the way that Gene reacted to his family. Like, she probably wouldn't have known them very well herself, so she was simply going off what Gene said, or the way he acted towards them. I don't know, like I said, it's just how it felt to me.'

'I concur,' said Wade, shocking the female passengers with an unsolicited, if brief, statement.

'Great guts think alike, it seems,' Shaw deadpanned.

Rawiri James lived in a small flat above a kebab shop. The perfect spot for a musician who does a lot of late-night gigs.

He opened his door, and gave a start when he noticed Dana lurking behind the police officers.

'Oh, I didn't know you were with the force too,' he remarked. 'You're certainly versatile!'

Dana laughed. 'It's just a temporary gig.'

'I know how that feels,' said Rawiri.

'Right! Yeah, I'm just the guitar-related advisor for this case.'

Rawiri's expression clouded over at the reminder of the reason for their visit. 'Gotcha. Please, all of you, come in.'

In a scenario to which Dana was swiftly becoming accustomed, they were ushered into the lounge and offered a cup of tea, just as Stephanie had done. The differences in this case were that Rawiri's lounge was tiny, and his teacups chipped and battered, but he made up for it by also offering them some nice chocolate biscuits, which were gratefully, even ravenously, accepted.

Shaw was right, Dana thought, this interviewing

is hungry work.

The guitarist's flat was ramshackle but clean; his sofa old and sagging, but comfortable. Like Stephanie, Rawiri also had a guitar close to hand, all the better to pick up and play at a moment's notice, Dana assumed. His instrument was on a good sturdy guitar stand, and next to it was a pedalboard and a powerful but portable amplifier. Larger than Stephanie's practice amplifier, but small enough for one person to lug to and from gigs without needing help.

Under Constable McNeish's expert guidance, Rawiri laid out his version of the events of the night of Gene's murder. It tallied with Stephanie Ngata's, right down to the general vibe that things were not great in the Stevens household.

'I'd only recently begun taking lessons from Gene. The only time I ever laid eyes on his wife, she saw me coming in, took one look at my guitar case, sneered at it, then stalked out of the house,' said Rawiri. 'And Devon was more interested in tinkering with his car in the shed – sorry, The Stables, pretentious twat – than playing guitar. Which is a shame, because they say he was actually a gifted player back in the day.'

'Who was saying this, exactly?' Wade asked.

'Oh, some of the other students. We have a get-together, like a big jam, every few months. I'd just started lessons when they had the most recent one. The students who've been with Gene for years tell you stuff like that. Some of them were taking lessons back when Devon was, too. This would have been, oh, I guess when he was twelve or thirteen maybe?'

Dana nodded. That would have been around the time she used to see Devon accompany Gene to industry events. Being shown off to the company reps.

Wade asked if he could have a quick look around the flat. Rawiri said 'You've had the grand tour, basically.' He pointed to a corner of the room. 'There's the kitchen. You're sitting in the lounge, cum dining room, cum recording studio, haha. There's only the bedroom and bathroom left, just down the corridor.'

Wade nodded to him, and got up from his seat.

'If you get lost, just ask the butler for directions,' said Rawiri. Dana chuckled dutifully at that quip, but the officers were all business, and completely ignored it.

Detective Shaw inhaled a chocolate biscuit and then took the reins of the interview.

'Can you think of anyone who would want to do harm to Mr Stevens?'

'No,' said Rawiri. 'I mean, he could be a grumpy old bugger, but that's hardly a reason to kill someone, is it?' He thought for a minute. 'Stephanie looked a bit upset when she left the place, as I was going in. But he was still alive then, so obviously she didn't kill him.'

'Upset?' said Shaw. 'Could you tell us more about that?'

Rawiri looked at his shoes. 'Oh, look, I told you I didn't know the guy very well, right? So maybe this is just all gossip and bullshit, but...'

He tapered off, but Shaw tapped her pen on her pad, bringing his attention back, and subtly reminding him that the visit was an official, important one.

He cleared his throat and continued. 'Okay. Well, at the jam session, I heard a few things floating around, like sometimes Gene might spend a bit of extra time showing some of the women how to hold a chord shape on the guitar neck, that kind of thing. As in, he had been known to go and stand in behind some of the students and reach his arms around them to ah... help them into the correct position.'

Rawiri's cheeks were going bright red. 'But, as I said, I never saw anything like that happen, and maybe someone was spreading rumours for some other reason, who knows? So, maybe Gene had done something to Stephanie that night, or maybe she'd just had a text message with some other bad news. All I know is that she looked upset.'

Dana nodded, but sagely left the talking to the Detective this time.

Shaw noted all this down, then shifted in her seat, and changed tack with her questions. 'Were you acquainted with Nikau Daniels at all?'

Dana knew that name from somewhere. Where had she heard it recently? Oh yes, Nikau was the guitarist from Audible Marks, the band she'd seen at the gig with Brody the other night.   She wondered where Shaw might be going with this.

'Oh, yes, I met him once or twice.' Rawiri flicked some invisible crumbs off his knee. 'Pretty flash guitar player,' he grunted.

Dana schooled herself not to allow a smile at the sound of a grown man being forced to acknowledge the skills of a much younger guitarist.

Shaw continued. 'Nikau was the last student Gene met with on the night he was killed. The last student to see him alive.'

She let that sink in for a minute.

'So, I just wondered if you had an opinion of him, or if you knew if he got on well with Gene or not.'

'Well, jeez, everyone found Gene a little gruff, like I said,' replied Rawiri, looking shocked. 'But nobody would want to kill him.'

'Somebody obviously did,' said Shaw, subtle as a thrown brick. Dana knew her well enough by now to know that she could tread softly when she wanted to, so presumably this was an interviewing technique designed to rattle something out of Rawiri. Dana wondered if that meant she truly suspected Nikau to be the killer, or perhaps the fact she was trying to rattle Rawiri meant she thought he'd done it? A third possibility occurred to Dana. Perhaps she was overthinking all this based on watching too many TV shows, and Shaw's question was nothing more than it appeared. Phew, it was exhausting trying to keep all of this straight!

For her part, Dana couldn't imagine Nikau killing Gene. But, once again, she had to admit that part of that impression was based on the fact that she simply couldn't imagine anyone who played guitar as sublimely as Nikau doing something as horrible as murder.

'Well, again,' said Rawiri, 'I can only go on the few brief times I've hung out with people, but Nikau seems like a real gentle soul. You know, he's as quiet as a mouse until you hand him a guitar and get him onstage. Then he becomes a rampaging beast.'

Shaw raised an eyebrow at that description. 'A

rampaging beast, you say?' She wrote something in her notebook.

'Oh hey,' Rawiri protested. 'I just meant he was an extrovert on the stage, that's all!'

He looked to Dana with a pleading expression, and although she knew exactly what he meant, she wished he'd used a different turn of phrase.

Dana was sure that Detective Shaw knew that too, so she once again managed to keep quiet. She was getting good at this!

Wade re-entered the room, and Shaw wrapped things up with a 'Thanks for your time' to Rawiri, and then they were out of there, leaving him stewing in his own juices. Although Dana contrived to be the last one out the door so she could flash him an encouraging smile on the way out.

***

'Congratulations, Miss Osborne,' said Shaw once they were back in the car. 'You performed commendably well in that interview.'

Dana knew that sounded like a compliment but was actually Shaw-speak for 'thanks for shutting the hell up'. Still, she had worked quite hard at it, so she took the win.

'Why were you so aggressive with Rawiri?' she

asked.

'You mean, the suspect?'

'No, I mean Rawiri James, the chilled-out guitar player who had no grudge against Gene, and wasn't even the last to see him alive.'

Shaw nodded. 'Okay, fair point.' She put her seatbelt on and signalled Wade to head off to the next interviewee. 'You see, Miss Osborne, it's most likely that one of Mr Stevens' students is the murderer. Rawiri James was looking a bit too relaxed for my liking. I thought I'd see if he was easily riled. Maybe something Gene said set him off, and he returned later that evening to take his revenge, who knows?'

'It wasn't him.'

'Well, thank you for engaging your psychic powers and making our job so much easier,' said Shaw. 'I don't know why we never called you in earlier. Would have saved us all a lot of time, since you can tell whether someone's guilty just by looking at them.'

'You know I'm right, though, don't you?' said Dana, getting a little hot under the collar. 'You don't seriously think he did it?'

Shaw harrumphed a bit, and shifted in her seat. Eventually she said 'It doesn't seem likely that he did it, but we simply can't rule anybody out at this time. You understand that, right? I'm not saying he definitely did it, I'm just saying we have to keep an open mind.'

Dana turned and stared out the window.

Keeping an open mind was not as much fun as it might sound.

***

The remaining interviews went the same way. Chat chat chat, the interviewee tells them how Gene Stevens was grumpy but an okay guy, Wade leaves the room for a poke around, Shaw attempts to jog extra information loose, Shaw fails to do so, they have copious cups of tea and the odd biscuit, and then leave.

Nikau Daniels was the last on the list, and his interview basically conformed to the pattern. Yes, he was the last person with a lesson that night. But it was clear that he looked up to Gene, almost idolised him.

'He was the first guy to give me a chance,' said Nikau. 'Most people take a look at me, think I'm worth nothing. Young Maori kid out to make trouble, is what they see. Think I'll never amount to anything. That's what my teachers at school actually used to say to me.'

Nikau stared defiantly at Shaw, as if daring her to voice the same opinion.

She said nothing, so he continued. 'If I go into Guitarz Guitars, the sales staff watch me the whole time, like I'm going to nick off with something.' He sneered. 'A white kid goes in, grabs a guitar off the wall to have a play, nobody bats an eyelid. Shit, I didn't even have a guitar at home, I used to have to wait for lunch breaks at school, just so I could play on the old piece of crap guitar that they had in the music room there.' His expression softened. 'Then Gene visited the school one day, to advertise his guitar lessons. I knew there was no way my mum could ever afford anything like that for me. But he saw how keen I was, and he took me on for free. He trained me up, got me into bands, got me writing songs. He had a plan…' Nikau hung his head. His hands were balled into fists on his lap.

'A plan?' prompted Shaw, so gently I had to look and check it was her speaking.

Nikau raised his head. 'Yeah, a plan. He was going to help me make money out of my music. He said he thought I could potentially be a star, but even if that didn't happen I could still make good money, and help my mum. I could play covers gigs, give lessons myself one day, do sessions and play guitar on other people's songs, all that.'

He shook his head, and wiped away a tear. 'But now he's gone. The only guy who ever gave a shit about me.'

***

After they'd left Nikau's house and got back into the car, Dana was still struggling to reconcile the different faces of Gene Stevens that they'd heard about today.

To most people, he was a grumpy, pushy, potentially creepy guy, who rubbed them up the wrong way, but got the job done.

But to Nikau, he was a proper mentor and life coach, with a generous streak.

This whole thing was getting overly complicated. If it was just a matter of finding the guitar and there's your killer, that would be straightforward. But trying to figure it out based on people's reactions to the man just gave you way too many suspects, plus one person who worshipped him.

Wade dropped her off back at the shop, with Shaw promising to call her the next day with any updates.

The shop was already closed, but Brody was still there, waiting to report on the day's activities.

Turns out he'd been successful in selling another

guitar, and this time it was one of the mid-range ones, a significantly more expensive model than the beginner's package he sold that morning.

Brody was practically vibrating with excitement, and insisted on re-enacting the whole sale for her. It seemed he had memorised the entire conversation from the second the customer had stepped into the store.

Dana was wrung out, and really only wanted to head upstairs, put on Blizzard of Ozz, or maybe something by Christine and the Queens, and relax in the bath.

But oh, how could she do that to Brody? It's not that she felt she had to mother him or anything, it was just that his excitement was contagious, and she found herself drawn into the fascinating Saga of The Customer Looking For Their First Decent Guitar, Parts One to Three.

She drew up a stool, leaned against the wall under the poster of her brother, and let Brody's account of his mundane triumph soothe away her busy thoughts. He was an entertaining storyteller, she had to hand it to him.

Although, as the Bard of Business Transactions drew to his conclusion, she found that the bit about the customer's credit card being rejected initially because of an incorrect PIN was, frankly, not as scintillating as the rest of the story, and Dana started yawning.

'Sorry!' said Brody. 'OMG, you're probably real tired, and here I am prattling about selling a guitar to someone, as if it's the first time it's ever happened.'

Dana almost said that she knew it was only the second time it had ever happened, but hey, it seemed like every time she left him to run the shop he made a sale, so she wasn't complaining.

'Please don't apologise,' said Dana. 'If there's any story I like to hear, it's one where the shop is doing well. I am tired though, so I'm going to head upstairs and hit the hay, okay?'

'Sure thing. See you tomorrow!'

Once he'd left, she realised she was too tired to go through the whole bath routine. Instead she just ended up feeding Paws McCartney, then stood in front of the fridge forking some cold leftover lasagne into her mouth, and finally collapsed into bed.

She slept, and she dreamed. She dreamed about being at a gig with Brody. It was the gig they'd attended the other night. She relived the support band's set. This Plastic Happiness. They were a tighter band in her dream. The dream drummer had obviously been practicing hard.

She wondered why she was here. It was unusual for her to have a lucid dream. Maybe she was supposed to do something, or change something. But as much as she concentrated, she remained a passenger, watching the dream unfold almost as if she was back at the gig.

Oh well, at least the next band was a good one. Nikau Daniels' band: Audible Marks. She'd happily relive that set, as long as the dream let her get some rest after that.

In the dream, This Plastic Happiness finished their set and left the stage, with the bass player catching up with Brody afterwards, just like he had in real life.

When Audible Marks tools the stage, suddenly it all made sense.

She saw the band file out onto the stage, instruments in hand. She looked at Nikau. Looked at his guitar.

Time froze, then the tableau shattered into a million pieces.

She woke, breathless, heart pounding.

Nikau had been playing Gene's Draydon Weka.

CHAPTER 12

It was exactly one cup of coffee past midnight, and Dana had worn a groove in her carpet from pacing. She was thinking hard. More accurately, she was stressing out.

There was no way she could go back to sleep after the dream she'd just had. Her subconscious brain had clocked the details that her waking mind hadn't taken in at the time she attended the gig with Brody. And now it had demanded her attention, and replayed the gig for her.

Now she looked back on it, it was obvious. The marks of age that Nikau had made on his cheap guitar to make it look like an old one. They were real. It wasn't a cheap, new guitar pretending to be an old one. He was using an actual 1961 Draydon Weka. And, going from the photo's she'd seen of Gene Stevens' guitar, she was confident it was his one.

Well, she would find out for sure once she called

the police and they went to have a look.

She mentally kicked herself. She should have been the one to look around Nikau's house, not Wade. He wouldn't know a classic guitar from a bag of spanners. He probably walked right past it.

No, that's not fair. Wade would surely have asked Dana to check any guitars he found in Nikau's house, so it mustn't have been there. Left in a rehearsal room or something, perhaps.

But why did Nikau have that guitar? She still found it hard to imagine that Nikau could have killed Gene. Was all of Nikau's talk about Gene being an amazing mentor just play-acting?

If Nikau had done it, surely he would know that he couldn't get away with it forever. Especially if he was taking the guitar out to gigs. Dana paused her pacing for a second. There's no way he'd be so stupid as to kill someone, steal an extremely valuable guitar, and then take it out and play it in front of dozens of people.

Nikau didn't seem the monumentally stupid type.

In that case, maybe he was an evil genius, and had decided to hide in plain sight.

Dana feet decided to resume their pacing, while her brain was busy with all these thoughts.

She sighed. There was no use putting it off any

longer. She had to call Wade, and let him decide what to do.

She couldn't shake the feeling that nobody who could play guitar that well could possibly be a murderer. She knew it didn't make any sense, but that was how she felt. Was she just letting her sympathy for the young, disadvantaged boy cloud her judgement? Was he playing her, just as masterfully as he played guitar?

She shook it off, and picked up her phone.

***

Ten more minutes of nervous pacing later, Wade and Detective Shaw were at her flat, picking her up to go to Nikau's house.

Wade's face was sleep-creased and his eyes were bleary. Dana supposed she didn't look any better. And she'd had the devil of a time figuring out what clothes to wear when going to possibly arrest someone. It was easy for the officers, they had uniforms. Dana had gone with jeans and a navy puffer jacket. Closest she could get.

Shaw looked the same as she ever did. All steel and determination. Her cropped hair stood on end - maybe she ordered it to stand to attention every morning? Dana could imagine her having that kind of self-control.

The mood was sombre in the car. Dana thought the officers might be excited to think they might have solved the case. But maybe they were also sad that it was Nikau they were preparing to visit.

By the time they got to his house, it was one o'clock in the morning. Dana felt uncomfortable about knocking on someone's door at that time. You always know it will be bad news, don't you?

Wade knocked a few times, but there was no answer.

'He might have legged it?' Wade suggested to Detective Shaw.

She nodded. 'Maybe. Pop round the back and have a look through the windows, will you?'

'Are we going to smash his door down?' asked Dana.

Wade and Shaw stared at her.

'What?' said Shaw. 'No, we are not going to smash his door down. Jeez, this isn't Starsky and Hutch, Miss Osborne. We'd need a warrant to get inside the house. Even looking through the windows is a grey area, and we're only doing it to confirm that Nikau hasn't hurt himself.'

Wade raised an eyebrow at this. Shaw jutted her chin at him and sent him on his way. He shrugged, and did as he was told.

Dana shoved her hands in her jacket pockets and watched her breath frost in front of her face. She looked over at Shaw, seemingly unaffected by the temperature.

'How are you not freezing right now?' she asked.

Shaw winked – yes, actually winked! – at her, and fished a tiny bag out of her pocket. 'Hand warmers.' She waved it at her. 'Never leave home without them. Especially on these night time jobs.'

By the time Wade returned, Dana was just starting to wonder if she could wrestle Shaw to the ground and steal a hand warmer from her. The odds were slim, but she was getting desperate.

Wade shook his head. 'Can't see any sign of him. I think he's scarpered. Our interview must have scared him off.'

'Dammit,' said Shaw. 'Radio it in, will you? And let's get our consultant back in the car while she's still a nice healthy blue colour.' She cast her eye over Dana. 'It's when you get to purple you're really in trouble.'

'Wait,' said Dana.

'You'd prefer to stand around outside?'

'Oh god no! For goodness' sake, let's get back in the car and get the heater on. No, what I meant was, wait before you radio it in.'

'Why's that?'

Dana slid into the back seat of the car, and fished out her phone. She tapped at it with numb fingers. 'I just had an idea of where he might be… aha! Yep.'

'What's the story?' said Wade. 'You're tracking him on your phone?'

'Kind of.' Dana showed her phone to the officers. 'I just looked up his band page. They're playing at The Duck 'n' Cover tonight.'

Shaw looked impressed. 'Good detecting, Miss Osborne. Wade, get us to the pub, please.'

With the car's heater on full, Dana's ears burned as the blood flow returned to them. By the time they got to the Duck 'n' Cover, she was very nearly back to normal temperature, and then it was only a quick run from the car into the toasty warm venue.

Judging by the way there were still a few punters at the bar, and the background music was still pumping through the big PA rather than the house sound system, Dana guessed that the main act had only recently vacated the stage. She hoped that Nikau and his band were still backstage, otherwise poor old Wade would have to drive them back to Nikau's house, where they'd just been.

The bar manager approached Detective Shaw with a worried look on his face.

'Everyone's been checked for ID, Detective,' he

said. 'We've had no trouble tonight.'

'Is that why you sent your offsider to check who's in the toilets?' Shaw replied.

The bar manager gulped. 'If there's anything going on in there, it's nothing to do with me.'

Shaw nodded. 'No stress, mate. We're only here to have a chat with one of the band members. Can you show us where the band area is, please?'

A very relieved pub manager quickly ushered them out of the main bar, down a shabby corridor and into a somewhat derelict back room. The salubrious Green Room of performing artist legend. Famous artists could expect a healthy buffet, copious whistle-whetting fluids, comfy chairs, and pleasant surroundings. Up-and-coming bands playing the Duck 'n' Cover could expect a tiny room with bare walls, and, if they were lucky, a rickety table to put their beers on. Beers they'd had to buy themselves, out of the performance money they'd just earned. It was a pretty good arrangement really. For the bar owner.

The members of Audible Marks were all in the room, having a celebratory after their set, and hanging out with the other bands. Networking, it was called. Not 'getting drunk in the shabby room out the back'. No, this was an important part of being in a band. Not so much the drinking part. Just getting to know other musicians, sharing information about venues and gigging opportunities, and crafting alliances for future gigs and tours.

You didn't have to drink alcohol to do that. Dana reflected that times had moved on, since bands toured in the Seventies and Eighties. Back then, it was expected that musicians would get wrecked and cause trouble. Nowadays, bands were more savvy, career-focused, and — crucially, in the beginning phase — usually didn't have a record company paying their expenses. In this DIY atmosphere, every band member knew the cost of a drink because they paid for it.

Having said that, the manager of the Duck 'n' Cover knew a good thing when he saw it, so if a band brought in a good crowd, he'd shout them a drink or two. Then it was just a matter of arguing over who'd be driving the van home.

Amongst the scrum of musicians in the room, Dana spotted Nikau. He was in the far corner, still noodling on his guitar. Well, Gene's guitar, if she had guessed correctly.

God, he reminded her of Ziggy. Never went anywhere without a guitar in his hand. It didn't have to be plugged in, because it wasn't always about making a loud noise. Sometimes it was just about working the muscle memory into the fingers. Sometimes it was a security blanket. Sometimes it was just that it felt good to be holding something as cool as a guitar.

Nikau looked happy and relaxed. That was about to change.

With a flick of her eyes, Shaw sent Wade to get Nikau.

As soon as the officer entered the room, everyone froze.

It's true that even nice, normal, law-abiding citizens can sometimes get a fright when a police officer appears out of nowhere. Even when they know they've done nothing wrong.

Now, multiply that feeling by a thousand, and you begin to understand what it's like when a room full of musicians sees an officer of the law. As a trainee rock'n'roll rebel, if you spend long enough cultivating an anti-establishment image, you can start to believe it.

Studies show that only a vanishingly small percentage of musicians actually have a past life as a drug-dealing gang member with a passion for stolen cars, and a bullet scar on their cheek. But they all react the same when 'the five oh' turn up. Honestly, Dana had even heard a trust-fund cowboy guitarist use the term 'five oh' once. It was cringeworthy.

Watching all these fine young people freak out as Wade walked amongst them would have been funny, if Dana hadn't known the purpose of the visit.

Nikau frowned. Given his mistrust of authority figures, and what he'd told them about being profiled in the past, Dana didn't blame him. He was perhaps the only person in the room who was justifiably concerned about their visit. And perhaps that's why he was the only one there who looked not only worried, but also resigned.

Wade went over and talked to Nikau. Every single other person in the room subtly shifted as far away as possible, while simultaneously keeping away from Shaw in the doorway. It was complex mathematics, calculating the best ratio of empty space to police officer, and a few people bumped into each other as their computations went awry, like a bad break on the pool table.

To their credit, Nikau's bandmates stuck by him. There were mutterings of 'you can't do this', and 'where's your warrant?', and even one barely audible 'bloody pigs', which Wade did a great job of pretending not to hear.

But when Wade duly produced the warrant for Nikau's arrest, there wasn't much more the bandmates could do, apart from promise to help get him free.

The guitar was removed from his hands, and although one of his mates tried to take possession of it, Wade made it abundantly clear that the instrument should be given to Dana. She made sure to grab the correct case for it. She didn't want to cause an even bigger mess by mixing things up further. Although the actual original case was back at the police station, Nikau's one would keep it nice and safe until they could be reunited.

Nikau was taken to the car, and was distinctly not read his rights because they weren't in the United States. Dana was surprised and, if she was honest, a bit disappointed to find out that one of the seemingly essential pieces of police theatre did not apply in this jurisdiction.

In fact, Wade didn't even handcuff Nikau. On reflection, Dana decided that she preferred this more relaxed, real life, New Zealand way of doing things, even if it wasn't as exciting as what you saw on TV shows. She was sure she wouldn't enjoy living in a place where people were stuffing their pants with guns on a regular basis.

Finally, off they went, leaving the musicians in the back room of the Duck 'n' Cover inventing possible reasons for Nikau's arrest, the theories getting more elaborate and far-fetched as they chugged their way through the post-gig bottles of beer.

***

In the back seat of the car, the atmosphere was awkward, to say the least. There was Dana, holding Nikau's guitar case, while Nikau sat on the other side of the car, apparently oblivious as to the reason for his arrest.

'What's all this about, anyway?' he demanded. 'Someone report a brown face hanging around the white part of town again, or something?'

'That's not it at all, and I'm sure you know it,' replied Shaw. 'You've been playing gigs with a murder victim's guitar. You're also the last person to see him alive. What do you have to say about that, smartarse?'

Nikau's jaw dropped. 'Whoah, whoah, whoah! Gene lent his guitar to me. Are you seriously accusing me of stealing a dead man's axe?'

'It's worse than that, I'm afraid,' said Dana softly.

'What do you mean, worse than…oh.' A stunned silence filled the car as Nikau realised just how much trouble he was in.

'You can tell us all about it at the station,' said

Shaw.

Dana spent the rest of the trip staring uncomfortably out the window as Nikau swore under his breath.

When they got to the station, the first order of business was for Dana to authenticate the guitar Nikau had been playing. It was immediately obvious to her that it was Gene's prized instrument, and the serial number tallied with what Devon had told them, but she still took her time and documented everything diligently. She knew that Nikau's future hinged on this evidence.

Once she'd officially concluded that it was the real vintage deal, Wade logged it with Geoff in the Evidence Room. Dana felt sorry for the beautiful guitar, having to rest in the wrong case, while the correct one was nearby, but Wade told her they had to leave everything as it was while the investigation continued. She reassured herself that Nikau's newer guitar case was really quite a good one, and the guitar would be safe and secure in it. Maybe that's why Nikau hadn't taken the old case. It looked cool, but probably offered less protection from the wear and tear of gigging life.

Dana knew she should probably stop anthropomorphising the instruments she came into contact with, but they each seemed to have their own personality. Each one played its own way, and generated different melodies and styles for the person playing it.

As far as she was concerned, a good instrument soaked up the musical spirit of whoever played it. Gene's '61 Draydon could probably just about play itself by now, she reckoned.

Wade collected her and led her to the interview room, where Nikau was glaring sullenly at the walls.

Shaw was already there, and once Dana and Wade were seated, she kicked off.

'So Nikau, why don't you tell us how you came to be in possession of Gene Stevens' very expensive vintage guitar?'

Nikau shrugged. 'Not much point, is there? You've already decided that I killed him, then nicked it.' Now he focused his glare on Shaw. 'That's about the story, isn't it? Poor Maori kid steals priceless guitar and kills the owner, but is so stupid that instead of hoofing it, he hangs around to perform in public with the stolen guitar. Have I got that right, officers?'

Shaw spread her hands on the table between them. 'I don't know, Nikau. You tell me. Is that what happened?'

'Of course it bloody isn't!'

'So what did happen? You have to help yourself here, son, by telling me everything. I'm not a mind-reader.'

'You aren't gonna believe me, so what's the point?' Nikau's right leg was jiggling up and down, and his nostrils were flaring with each forced breath as he clamped his mouth shut.

'Please, Nikau, just tell us,' said someone. Oh dear, thought Dana, I think it was me.

She braced herself for a tirade from Shaw, or at least to be told to leave the room and don't let the door slap your arse on the way out. But nothing happened. Shaw didn't even turn her head. It seemed like either Shaw was starting to trust her, or else she just thought it might be useful to have the local guitar shop owner chip in to the conversation.

As if reading her mind, the next words out of Nikau's mouth were: 'You run that little music shop, eh? Pick On Me?'

'Pick Me,' said Dana, for the five hundredth time since naming her store. Oh well, too late to change it now. She still liked it, anyway. The play on words between using a guitar pick, and the mental image of a guitar calling out to its destined owner, both appealed to her.

'It's good,' said Nikau. 'I mean, you don't have

tons of stuff there, but it's a good shop.'

Dana was thinking back to what he'd said about being profiled in other guitar shops, and desperately hoped she'd never done anything like that to him herself. She liked to think she treated everyone the same, but there's a reason it's called unconscious bias, after all.

'Thank you, Nikau, it means a lot to me that you like my shop. It's something I've worked very hard on.'

Nikau shrugged again. 'Yeah, it's good. You need more twin humbucker guitars in there, but apart from that it's okay.'

'Oh, really?' said Dana. 'You get more emotion out of a single-coil, didn't you know that?'

For the first time that day, Nikau smiled. 'Gene always said if you get a good humbucker, it has more expressiveness than any single-coil.'

Dana crossed her arms. 'Maybe if you own a set of original 1961 humbuckers, you can get away with saying things like that. But there aren't many people in that select group, as you're surely aware. In fact, Gene was the only one I know of.'

Nikau's face closed again, just like that.

Dana uncrossed her arms and leaned forward. 'Gene was good to you, wasn't he?'

Nikau nodded without looking up.

'So you need to do right by his memory, and tell us what happened. We're here to help.'

Nikau's head whipped up, his face in a sneer. 'You're with the police, and yet you say you're here to help?'

'I...' Dana didn't know what to say. She knew that she was here to help. She assumed Wade and Shaw were too, but she could certainly understand why Nikau might not believe that.

And, frankly, if he didn't give them a good story right now, it was their job to put him in jail.

'Please, Nikau? I'd really like to know what happened.'

He struggled with himself a bit more, but in the end he started talking. Whether it was because he thought there was a chance they'd believe him, or just to get his story out and officially noted down, she didn't know.

'I had my lesson that night,' he began, right leg still jiggling like mad. 'Gene gave me a hard time about not practicing the previous lesson well enough. But then I showed him some footage of my last gig. I'd been putting in some of the modal stuff he'd been showing me whenever I had a solo, and I could see he was chuffed with that. "Like spices", he said. "Add a little exotic flavour to your solos." So then he was all happy and chatting about stuff, and that's when he gave me his guitar. Swapped it with my one. And then I left. And he was fine then. And that's all.'

Shaw tapped a finger on the table.

'You had a chat.' Tap. 'He gave you a guitar worth as much as a house.' Tap. 'Then you left, and he was fine.' Tap. 'Anything you want to add to that story? I might need a leeeetle bit more detail to convince a judge, you see.'

Nikau rocked back in his chair. 'Yeah, just like I thought. You find it hard to believe that a young Maori boy didn't do anything wrong, don't you? Have you tried asking all the Pākeha people who were in and out of the house that night? Oh, no, you don't need to bother with that, because you got the perp right here.'

'Actually,' said Shaw, 'we interviewed everybody who was present that evening, no matter what their ethnicity. Lady Justice is colour-blind, after all.'

'Lady Justice is a colonial construct designed to keep indigenous people under the thumb, so excuse me if I don't bow down to her.' Dana was impressed with Nikau's delivery of this statement, and judging by the way the corners of Nikau's mouth turned up, he was impressed with himself too. No matter the depth of the shark-infested water a person was currently trying to wade through, one can still take pride in a finely-crafted turn of phrase.

Shaw leaned back in her chair, and left a pause in the conversation, like a quarter-note rest, and then:

'Dana? Do you have anything else you want to try here?'

Dana thought about it for a minute.

'Nikau, why didn't Gene give you the guitar case as well?'

He shrugged.

'It's just,' Dana continued, 'that it's a cool old case, and they kind of make a set together. So why did he separate them?'

'It wasn't gonna be for long,' said Nikau. 'He was only lending me the guitar until I could afford a good one myself. So he found a basic case for it, plain but tough. He said then maybe people wouldn't know it was a really flash vintage guitar inside and it would be less likely to get stolen.'

Shaw's sharp intake of breath, and Wade's nodding to himself were Dana's confirmation that she had unearthed a salient point.

'Earlier, you made it sound like he'd gifted it to you forever,' she said. 'You realise that loaning you the guitar is quite a different thing than giving it to you, right? It makes much more sense now.'

Nikau snorted. 'It doesn't make any difference either way, once the police see me with it. They still think I've nicked it anyway.'

'Maybe, young man, but now it's getting a bit more explainable.'

The tide of belief might be starting to turn, Dana thought, and perhaps some of those sharks were only dolphins after all.

'This is a good thing, for you,' Shaw continued. 'What else can you tell me? How long was the loan for?'

'Just until I could save up for a better guitar myself. My old SG kept going out of tune, and one of the pickups kept cutting out.'

'An SG?'

'Yeah, Epiphone SG. Got it from my mate Hamish, you can check with him if you want.'

'You didn't have a copy of a Weka, then?'

'Nah, I got an SG because of Angus Young.'

'Hmmm… okay,' said Dana. 'You know, the tuning stability can usually be fixed by –'

'Can we stay focused, please?' said Shaw, cutting in before Dana went off down a guitar tech rabbit hole.

She cleared her throat. 'Yeah, sorry. Um, so… Nikau. Once you'd got enough money for a new guitar, you were going to give back Gene's one, is that right?'

'Yep.'

'And Gene was quite happy with that arrangement?'

'Sure - he was the one who suggested it.'

'And his family were cool with it?'

'Not really anything to do with them, is it?'

'Well,' said Dana, 'it is a significant asset, so they do have an interest in it.'

Another shrug from Nikau. 'Mrs. Stevens wanted fewer guitars in the house, far as I could tell. As for Devon, he liked having them around, but he hadn't played in ages. He used to play that one, but for the last few years he kept himself busy with his cars, out in the shed.'

'Right then. Thank you, Nikau, that's been very helpful. Hasn't it, Detective Shaw?'

Shaw didn't respond, just kept her eyes on Nikau for a while, before abruptly getting out of her chair and saying: 'Someone will come to get you soon, Nikau.' Then she left the room, and Dana found herself being ushered out by Wade.

She looked back at Nikau just before the door shut on him. He was slumped in his chair, staring at the table in front of him. She hoped he could get out of there soon.

Out in the reception area, Shaw thanked Dana for her help.

'When do you think you might release him?' Dana asked.

'Release him?' said Shaw. 'Why would we do that?'

Dana was taken aback. 'Ah, didn't you hear what he said? Gene lent him the Weka. And his own guitar was an SG, so it's not the one used as the murder weapon, so where did the other one come from? And Gene was fine when he left the house that night.'

Shaw rolled her eyes. 'Spare my days, woman. Did it ever occur to you that a person might lie to save their skin?'

Dana could feel the blush spreading across her cheeks. 'Of course, but you don't actually think he's lying, do you?'

Shaw put a hand on a hip. 'You don't actually think he's telling the truth, do you?'

Dana tried the hand-on-hip thing, too, but didn't quite pull it off with as much authority as Shaw did. Still, she forged ahead. 'Yes, actually, I do. I think he's just a young guy caught in the wrong place at the wrong time.'

'With the wrong monumentally expensive guitar in his hands, and the wrong person dead after he was the last person to see them alive. Yes.' Shaw stuck out her bottom lip and made a real-life sad face emoji. 'Poor young guy. Better let him off, just in case.'

'I feel you're being flippant about a young person's right to justice here.'

'Well, I feel you're probably the most naive person I've ever met, and I think we won't be needing your assistance any more. Thank you for your time.'

With that, Shaw bustled off into a back room, leaving Dana with her mouth hanging open.

Wade went to say something to her, then thought better of it, and followed his superior out the door..

CHAPTER 13

Night had turned into morning, and it was almost time to open the shop. Dana walked home, giving herself time to cool down, but as she slammed the front door of Pick Me Guitars, she had to admit that she was still righteously steamed up about Nikau's fate.

The door rattled in its frame after her shove, and the bell above it whipped off its spring and went flying into a corner.

Brody stood frozen in the middle of the shop, mouth opening and closing like a confused goldfish. In the end, he let out a muffled yelp and retreated to the back room. 'Just doing a stock check!' he called out, then shut the door behind him. Dana could swear she heard him lock it too.

She growled. Denied an opportunity to vent to Brody, she left him to open the shop, and went upstairs to have a nice, calming cup of tea. As she sat on the couch she realised that her hands had overruled her brain, and poured her a finger of peaty whiskey instead. But by then it was way too late to get back up and boil the jug, so she rolled with it. Needs must.

Paws McCartney leapt onto her lap and initiated his complicated kneading and circling pattern before settling down. It was like dialling in the combination on a safe, and he couldn't rest easy unless the ritual was performed correctly. Dana found it soothing, if sometimes a little like being tenderised by a tiny, furry chef.

She took a sip of whiskey and let the liquid sit there for a while, feeling the burn on her tongue. Fumes roiled in her mouth and escaped her nostrils, as the peat and alcohol did its work. Only once it felt like the whiskey had stripped a layer or two off her tastebuds, did she finally swallow.

Her Gran had sworn by a nip of whiskey each night. Sometimes that would lead to another nip, and then the songs would come out, and the old stories. She was happy with it, though, and was never an angry drunk. She'd keeled over in her early sixties and passed away, just like that, out of the blue. Dana hoped she herself would do the same one day. The thought of clinging to life even if the quality was going downhill filled her with dread. Like listening to a favourite LP until it wore out, there was a point where you had to admit you'd had your fun, and now it was time to spiral into the runout groove.

She slugged the last of the dram, and tried to shake off these maudlin thoughts. Now wasn't the time for wallowing. Now was the time for action!

What could she do to help Nikau?

She was absolutely convinced that he was innocent. But she could also understand why Detective Shaw would see it otherwise. Dana needed to find a way to change her mind.

There was only one logical approach. The only way to get Nikau out of trouble was... to find out who actually killed Gene.

Dana gulped. Was she really thinking of doing her own sub-rosa investigation into the case? Off the books, with no official imprimatur?

Think seriously, she told herself. This is a murder we're talking about. If something goes wrong, you could get hurt.

But she couldn't let it drop. She couldn't leave Nikau in a cell, just because he was too convenient a suspect.

Decision made, she felt a lot better. Now that she had a goal, she only needed to work away at the steps to achieve it. Just like learning guitar, really.

First step: catch up on sleep. Running around like

a zombie wasn't going to help anyone. If she was going to become a private investigator, she planned on being a sharp one.

So she shuffled off to the bedroom, got into her private investigator jim-jams, and slumped into her private investigator bed, for some quality professional development time.

***

Some hours later, after a bit of sleep and some fresh slap, she felt vaguely human again. She bustled downstairs to check on Brody.

He eyed her warily, but didn't run away. The sleep had obviously been good for her. Also, she was no longer angry enough to break parts of the store. Hmmm. She'd better hunt down that bell and reattach it later…

'Hi, Brody. Sorry about earlier. I'd had some bad news.'

'Boss, I know I'm sometimes slow on the uptake, but even I managed to figure that out.'

Dana dipped her head in acknowledgment. 'Right, right. So, listen. I figured out where Gene's guitar was.'

'Wait, what?'

'Yep. We were looking right at it.'

'We were?'

'We sure were. At the gig you dragged me out to. I mean, at the gig we attended the other night.'

'Gene's guitar was there? I don't remember seeing a vintage Draydon.' Brody's eyes flicked up and to the left as he interfaced with the Random Access Memory part of his brain. All of his musical knowledge eventually migrated to permanent, long-term memory storage, but this gig was comparatively recent, so it was still lodged in his RAM.

Dana knew she should stop thinking of Brody as an android recently stranded on Earth, but it made interacting with him so much easier that it was a hard habit to break.

With a click and a whirr (in her imagination, anyway), Brody retrieved the memory he sought, and scrubbed through it. Dana went to make a coffee, and fed Paws.

When she returned to the shop, Brody's shocked expression told her that he'd figured it out.

'Nikau had Gene's guitar?'

Dana nodded and handed him a cup of the finest freeze-dried joe she could afford.

'But if he had the guitar,' Brody continued, ignoring the cup, 'people might think that he killed Gene.'

'People do think that,' said Dana, placing the coffee on the counter in front of Brody, ready for when he resumed normal service. Stop that, Dana!

'But if people think that he killed Gene, eventually the police might find out.'

'The police did find out.'

'But if the police find out, he might go to jail.'

Dana sipped her coffee and let Brody get there on his own.

'Oh.'

'Yeah.'

'You don't think he did it, though,' said Brody. 'Do you?'

Dana inhaled coffee steam for a minute while she pondered the gravity of what she was about to say. She'd always been respectful of the police, and it felt deeply weird to contradict them.

'No,' she eventually pronounced. 'I'm confident they've arrested the wrong person. The murder weapon is a fake Weka – a Bluff – but Nikau didn't have a Weka, he had an SG. So where's his guitar? And where did the fake come from? The police think I'm being naive, but I honestly think Nikau's not the murderer.'

'Phew! Me too. The innocent of murder thing, not the you being naive thing.'

Dana raised her cup to him. 'Thanks for the

clarification.'

'You're welcome,' said Brody-bot, immune to sarcasm. 'So, what are we going to do?'

She appraised the young shop assistant in front of her. Did she really want to drag him into this? On second thought: it sounded like he'd already dragged himself into it, and was there any way she could stop him from joining in when he found out what she was intending to do?

She squared her shoulders. All she could do was tell him what she was thinking of doing, and let him be an adult and decide for himself.

'I'm going to investigate this case myself, and find the actual murderer, then tell the police.'

'Oooh,' said Brody, his eyes lighting up like programmable LED par cans, twenty percent off at Pick Me Guitar Shop this month only.

'It will probably be dangerous.'

'Hmmm...' Brody slumped. He'd never shown a huge appetite for danger.

'We'll probably have to go to lots of gigs, and talk to lots of guitarists.'

'Ooooh! And then, when we track down the perp, we can yeet them into a prison cell!'

Dana nodded cautiously in response. She'd need to search up the definition of the word yeet later, but whatever it meant, it didn't sound like the kind of thing that Brody did on a regular basis. Nonetheless, she couldn't fault his passion for the project.

She'd recently discovered that young people's slang had moved on past her comprehension, but it had taken her about ten years to notice. Which meant she was already so far behind that there was no chance of catching up. All those times her parents had looked confused when she talked to them — now she was doing the same to Brody. The difference was that she employed Brody, he'd signed a contract with her and everything. So if she wanted to, she could make him explain himself, whereas a parent had no such leverage over a child. But she tried not to do that too often. It was a bad look for her, and tedious for Brody.

She didn't want to turn into the annoying old Aunty figure. Not yeet, anyway. Hmmm… that's probably not how she was supposed to use that word.

A customer came through the door silently, what with the bell still lying forlornly in the corner waiting for Dana to restore it to its rightful place and function.

'Okay Brodes. You look after this customer. I'll fix the bell. Then we'll suss out our plan of attack.'

Brody went for a high-five, but Dana backed away.

'No, Brody. You know I won't allow that here.'

Dana liked people, she really did. She just didn't gel with all the new-fangled ways of making physical contact with them. Her knowledge of such things was limited to a handshake for a greeting, and hugs on an as-required basis.

She reeled as a thought struck her. Oh my god, what if she was the Brody-bot?

'Fist bump?' said Brody, hopefully.

She shook her head. 'Honestly, that might even be worse.'

'Awww, come on!' he muttered as he sloped off to intercept his victim.

One fixed bell and one packet of strings sold later, Dana and Brody huddled together again for their mission-planning session.

'Okay, boss,' said Brody. 'What's your plan?'

'We're going to Meltdown Music.'

Brody's face lit up with a grin that could have powered half of the town's Festival of Lights.

***

Meltdown Music occupied a petite warehouse

three streets over from the Pick Me Guitar Shop. Well, warehouse was overstating it. Large shed was more accurate. Really, 'lockup attached to some guy's house' was the factually correct phrase. But, although it was small on the outside, it was big on the inside. Not in terms of spatial bigness, but in terms of being big with goodness.

The tiny shed had become the go-to place for second hand instruments. Not the uber-expensive ones that you'd find in The Vault at Zander's Rare Guitars, but all the quirky-yet-affordable ones that mainstream collectors hadn't latched onto. Plus a whole lot of straight up good guitars that might not set the world on fire with guitar-lust, but would perform consistently, and serve a musician well for the entirety of their gigging life. Dana had a special place in her heart for all the bog-standard Telecasters and their ilk. Guitars like that just kept making music year after year without any bells and/or whistles. Unless you attached a bell or a whistle to it. You could happily screw anything onto a plank of wood like a Tele, and it would keep on trucking.

Meltdown Music could kit out your band ready for any gig in any genre, and they'd do it cheap, and they'd do it from what was in stock that day. And no, before you ask, none of the gear was stolen. The owner, Gordon Butler, just happened to be really good at spotting bargains. He also knew all the musicians, and because he'd given so many of them a great deal when they were starting out, he was their main guy to sell old gear to, and they usually returned the favour by not asking too much on the return journey. In this way, the interconnected family tree of musicians in town helped each other out, and kept the groove going across generations.

Dana knew a lot of people in the local scene, but Gordon knew everyone. And, because he travelled out of town for buying trips, he knew people all around the country. And, because he dealt in second-hand instruments, he'd also been ripped off several times by assholes. People who might, for example, try to make a cheap guitar look like a more expensive one, so they could get more money for it.

Gordon's memory was capacious, and with all his contacts, those rip-off artists usually got payback at some later date. Gordon was unhurried. He took the long view, and waited for situations to get to a tipping point, where he could give a gentle nudge so that things balanced out again.

If there was anyone who could tell Dana where a mysterious Bluff guitar fake had sprung from, and what demented Frankenstein might have created it,

Gordon was not just top of the list: he was the list.

Added bonus: if anyone knew what had become of the road crew from Ziggy's last tour, it was Gordon. A visit with him might bring Dana one step closer to piecing together her brother's last hours, and finding out what low-life scum had taken his guitar.

Extra added double bonus: her and Brody got to visit the coolest little guitar emporium, and talk gear with a fellow enthusiast.

Gear-nerd time!

CHAPTER 14

This operation was deemed important enough that Dana had actually closed the shop for the afternoon. Now that her and Brody had formed a crack two-person investigation team, the shop would have to remain unattended while they did their sleuthing.

Brody was intent on coming up with a name for their detecting duo.

His list included the following:

- Pick Me! Guitar Investigation Unit
- Guitar Crimes Inc.
- Fret-Related Incident Examination Nimble Detective Squad (FRIENDS for short)
- Covert Guitar Ops

Dana preferred The Fret Detectives herself, but she let Brody chatter on while she hauled open the door of the garage out the back of the shop, and attempted to coax her poor, neglected old VW Beetle into life.

With a groan and a splutter, eventually the car kicked into action, and the air was filled with the somewhat flatulent sound of the rear-mounted 1300cc engine.

Possibly the least useful vehicle for a musician, the Beetle had just enough room for a guitarist and her gear, but only if the gear was one guitar and a very small amplifier. Plus it had better not be heavy, because the tiny engine would struggle to go uphill with anything heavier than a travel blanket on the back seat.

As a kid, she had climbed all over her grandmother's vintage VW like it was a purpose-built play area rather than a mode of transportation. Beetles filled her with warm feelings of comfort and love, even as they rattled and froze her. Real life can't compete with sentimental memories.

The creaky old vinyl seats were starting to split at the seams, and there were so many leaks that the inside air was basically just outside air in the shape of a VW, but Dana loved her Beetle. From its spindly gearstick to its oh-so-cute little glovebox, the car was her absolute favourite non-guitar-related item.

She waved Brody into the car – he was still brainstorming detective names, he hadn't stopped this whole time – and they blatted off down the road.

'Wait up,' said Brody, as they beetled along, with the mountain ranges south of Rockingham West forming a towering backdrop to the town. Impressive as they were, Brody's attention was on something inside the car. 'What's that thing?' He pointed down in between the seats.

'What? The gearstick?'

'I guess. Why do you keep having to shove it backwards and forwards like that?'

Dana glanced at him sideways while trying to watch the road.

'I'm changing gears, Brody.'

He was silent for a few seconds.

'Doesn't it do that for you?'

Dana chuckled. 'No, actually Brody, a lot of older cars are manual. You have to do the thinking and all of the driving for yourself.'

He sucked in a breath between his teeth and made a face like he'd just drank a glass of water that turned out to be lemon juice.

'Seems incredibly risky, trusting humans to do all that.'

Dana went to object, but then thought about it. She had to concede that he had a point.

'It's kinda fun though,' she eventually said.

'Is it really?'

'Yeah. You do all these things and the car goes. It's like a test of your manual dexterity.'

'Well, if you put it that way,' said Brody, 'you can count me out, for sure. I want a vehicle that doesn't test me at all. I want a car that's so user-friendly that I could fall asleep while driving and I'd still wake up safely at home.'

'Maybe we should listen to the radio for a bit,' said Dana, valiantly attempting to change the subject.

'The what?!' said Brody, poking at the dashboard. 'I thought that was a kids' toy or something. Who listens to the radio?'

Dana shifted in her seat. 'People with old cars, I guess,' she muttered.

'Did you just say "old people with cars?"' Brody giggled.

Dana ground her teeth, and cranked the AM so she wouldn't have to hear any more of Brody's witticisms as she drove.

It was a fine afternoon and all the residents of Rockingham West were out mowing the lawns, in order to qualify for an early beer o'clock. You do the mahi, you get the treats, after all.

The old VW pootled past kiddies sitting on the berm trying to sell feijoas. The odd kindly citizen stopped to buy a couple, even though feijoas were practically clogging up the stormwater drains this time of year. It was good to encourage the young people to try to sell them, if only to keep the kids – and the fruit – from making a nuisance of themselves all over the place.

***

They got to Meltdown Music without Brody falling out of the car by accident after mistaking the door handle for a console game controller or anything, so Dana chalked it up as a win.

Gordon had obviously heard the old VW coming because he was waiting at the door to his establishment with a big grin on his face.

His bear-like frame almost obscured the whole doorway; his shaggy beard could have been the welcome mat, grabbed up off the ground and glued to his chin.

'Dana!' he cried. 'Haven't seen you in donkeys. Come here!' He enveloped her in a hug, and raised his eyebrows in greeting at Brody.

'Hi Gordon,' said Dana. 'This is my shop assistant, Brody.'

'Partner, actually,' said Brody. 'I'm Dana's partner in a private investigation firm called Lutherie Sleuths.' He shook the big man's hand after he'd released Dana.

'Lutherie Sleuths,' said Gordon, nodding. 'Cool name.'

'I don't know if that is our name, actually,' said Dana, flicking a side eye at Brody. 'I thought we were still mulling it over. I was going for Fret Detectives.'

Gordon nodded again. 'Also cool. If you guys can't decide on one, at least you have some potential band names there.'

'Oh, true!' said Brody. 'Dana, maybe we should write a theme song!'

'Yep, that's a good idea, Brodes.' She had to admit to herself she'd been wrong. Brody wasn't a robot. He was a very affectionate, overgrown puppy. A Lab-Brody-doodle. 'For now, let's focus on why we're here.'

'Oh,' said Gordon. 'That sounds very official. What, indeed, is your purpose here today at the Shed of Shred?' He spoke out the side of his mouth to Brody. 'Get it? Guitarists who play a lot of notes real fast are called shredders, and here's my shed full of guitars. Shed of Shred. Cool, huh?'

'Haha! Yeah! Good one, Mr. Gordon.'

'Cheers. Why don't you both come in and tell me what's up?'

They followed Gordon into the unprepossessing

shop. It honestly looked like a large but boring, ordinary garden shed, squatting next to his house. Once inside, however, the Fret Detectives' – or maybe Lutherie Sleuths' – eyes lit up as they beheld the ragged glory of Meltdown Music.

Gordon was a magpie and he'd constructed a nest of affordable musical instruments. Displayed on hangers, stuffed into corners, shoved onto high shelves, a multitude of music-making apparatus bedecked the interior. The lemony smell of fretboard oil combined with that particular odour of burning dust you get when a valve guitar amp has been run hot for an hour, along with base notes of the lining from an old guitar case, and – what was that? – oh, a well-used drum throne. Ergh.

Dana edged away from the noisome item, and found a good corner with a counter to lean on while surveying the musical smorgasbord.

Brody didn't fare so well - he was offered the offending drum throne to sit on, but he didn't seem to notice the smell. He was gazing around the shed with his mouth hanging open. The optical stimulation must be overriding the olfactory assault.

Gordon shuffled around and squeezed himself in behind the counter, plonked his elbows down on it and spread his hands, inviting Dana to explain her mission.

'Okay,' she began. 'We have a couple of questions that we're hoping you can answer.'

'A man's life depends on it!' interjected Brody.

'Is that true?' asked Gordon.

'Um… kind of,' said Dana. 'Well, he's more of a kid than a man, and he's been arrested, but they're hardly going to execute him, I think, Brody, are they?' She answered herself. 'No, they aren't.'

'Who's been arrested?' said Gordon. 'And how can I help?'

'You might have seen him around, actually. His name's Nikau, and he plays with the band Audible Marks.'

'Oh yeah.' Gordon straightened up and stuck his hands on his hips. He towered over the counter, his head almost brushing the ceiling. 'That kid is on fire. Great guitar player. What's he been arrested for?'

'The police think he killed Gene Stevens.'

'Well that's bullshit, for starters.'

'That's what we reckon, too,' Brody chimed in.

'I see him round here all the time. He's about the nicest, most gentle kid you'll ever meet. Wouldn't hurt a fly.'

'That's what we thought,' said Dana. 'But they found him with Gene's precious guitar –'

'Actually,' said Brody, 'you told the police he had it.'

Dana ground her teeth. Her face went all warm. 'I'm embarrassed to admit that's true,' she said. 'But I never thought that he'd be arrested for murder. I was simply trying to find out what had actually happened, and I thought that finding Gene's guitar might be part of the puzzle.'

'And now you think it's not?' asked Gordon.

'Correct. There was a fake version of Gene's Weka left at the scene – in fact, it was the murder weapon.'

'Shit,' said Gordon. 'That's cold.'

'You're damn right about that,' said Dana, with a shudder. 'Anyway, we initially assumed that the killer had stolen Gene's guitar, and swapped it for a fake, hoping that nobody would notice.'

'But Dana was too sharp for that,' Brody interrupted. 'She spotted the fake from a photograph.'

'Wow,' said Gordon. 'Really? You picked a Bluff from a photo? Good skills.'

'Thanks,' said Dana, blushing for a different reason now. 'Ahem. As I was saying, because of this, we thought that whoever had the real guitar must be the killer. But Nikau said he didn't steal the guitar, Gene lent it to him, and I believe him.'

'Me, too,' said Brody.

Dana sighed. 'We both believe that, yes. May I continue?'

Brody waved her on, magnanimously.

'Thank you,' she said, trying to suppress an eye-roll. 'Anyway, Nikau didn't swap his guitar with Gene's. Nikau had a cheap SG, not a Weka-style guitar, so the fake one at the crime scene isn't his. So where did the fake Bluff come from? There's obviously another person involved. And we think that person might be the killer. That's why we're here. We wondered if you know anyone who's making fakes like that, maybe trying to pass them off as vintage ones.'

She pulled out her cellphone and showed Gordon the photos of the fake guitar that she'd taken back at the police station when she'd examined it.

He swiped through the various shots, zooming in every now and then, pursing his lips and rubbing his chin thoughtfully.

He let out a long breath and then nodded.

'There's only one guy I know does work like that. Ray Cornelius over in the wine district.'

'Thanks,' said Dana. 'Wait… we have a wine district in RockWest?'

Gordon chuckled. 'No, it's a shop called The

Wine District. Cornelius makes things out of old wine barrels and sells them to rich people for tons of money. He's a bit of a genius with wood, actually. Knows his quarter-sawn wood from his…' Gordon waved a hand, '…wood that's not quarter-sawn. And all that stuff. I've seen him buy a new dresser from the furniture shop, throw some paint at it, scrape it off with a wire brush, then hit it with an old chain. Two days later it sold in his shop for five times what he paid for it.'

Dana wasn't sure she had the chutzpah to run a business on the premise of selling things that she'd purposefully wrecked. But having said that, she knew that distressed, or "road-worn" guitars commanded a premium, for reasons she couldn't fathom. It wasn't a look that appealed to her, so she rarely had them in her own shop, but if someone ordered one, she'd get it in for them.

'Okay, thanks for that Gordon. We'll go and pay him a visit.'

'Sure, but, I mean, don't just go and say "Hey, Gordon tells me that you will sometimes make a fake guitar in the hopes of swindling someone", right?'

'No, of course not! Don't worry, we'll be circumspect about it.'

'Yeah!' said Brody. 'Then, once we find out they

did it, we'll be all like slam! You're going to jail for murder, son!'

Gordon gave Dana a pleading look.

'It's all good,' she said, as she jerked a thumb towards Brody. 'I'll leave him in the car.'

Gordon looked immensely relieved at this news. Brody not so much.

'Hey! I was joking.'

'Okay Brody,' Dana pushed off the counter with her hip, and gave Brody a gentle shove to get him moving. 'Let's leave Gordon in peace now, shall we?'

'Oh, but can I just have a quick go on that little valve amp?' Brody begged, pointing at a diminutive noise machine that had probably already been a teen when Kurt Cobain passed away.

Dana crossed her arms and shot him a look. 'If it's okay with Gordon, you have two minutes.'

Brody, beaming, jumped up and wagged his nonexistent tail.

Gordon went to find a guitar cable while Brody picked out a test guitar.

'Actually, Gordon, I have one more question for you, if you don't mind?' said Dana.

'Shoot.'

'Do you know if any of the old road crew from Ziggy's last tour are still around town?'

'Oh. Um, let's see.' Gordon plugged the amplifier in and then thought for a bit.

'Yeah. Most of the crew graduated to bigger tours and then washed up in bigger towns. You know how the touring life is, you can end up becoming human flotsam, right? But I reckon there are a couple members of the crew still here. I'm sure I can find out within a day or so. Want me to get them to contact you?'

'Ah, could you maybe find out if they're around… without letting them know who's asking? And then just tell me?' Dana was aware how extra-dodgy this sounded, but she couldn't risk tipping them off, if one of them did indeed happen to be the person who'd stolen Ziggy's guitar.

Gordon looked at her with his head cocked to the side. 'Right,' he said eventually. 'Fret Detectives business, is it?'

Dana opened her mouth to reply, but before she could, Brody yelled out from the other side of the room, 'Lutherie Sleuths!'

Dana smiled at Gordon, and shrugged.

As she turned to collect Brody, Gordon put a gentle hand on her elbow.

'Hey, just quietly,' he said, leaning close, 'did you know that Rawiri James was having an affair with Gene's wife?'

Dana was taken aback. 'Rawiri and Maya? Really? He made it seem like Maya didn't think very much of him, when the police asked him about her.'

This was a lot for Dana to process. Being a private guitar investigator was turning out to, ipso facto, involve sifting through a lot of private information, and Dana wasn't usually one to gossip. But, she reminded herself, this wasn't about gossip — this was about motive for murder, and bringing the perpetrator to justice. So she swallowed her discomfort and got on with the job.

'Are you sure about that?'

'Absolutely positively,' Gordon replied. 'Had it from the horse's mouth, when said horse came in to look at a guitar.'

'He just told you about it?'

'He wasn't bragging, if that's what you're thinking. He looked more like he wanted to confess it to someone, and I happened to be handy.'

'When was this?'

'Last week, is when he told me. Said it had been going on for a week or two, and he said he thought Maya was ready to leave Gene. Again, he wasn't showing off. He said he got the impression she was ready to leave Gene anyway, not just to shack up with him.' Gordon shrugged. 'I don't know if that's helpful or not, but I thought you should know.'

'Yeah, it's definitely useful. Thanks, Gordon.'

'No problemo.'

Thus it was that they left Meltdown Music with a new lead on the fake Draydon, a new piece of information about Rawiri and his affair with Gene's wife Maya, and the hope of finding out which members of Ziggy's old road crew were still around. Oh, and a second-hand valve amp in the back seat. It had been too much of a funky old bargain piece for Brody to resist. He was sitting in the back seat, cuddling it, while Dana drove.

'Hey! Whoah!' he called out as she negotiated a pothole. 'Take it easy over the bumps, please, boss. Precious cargo here in the back.'

Dana was preoccupied with juggling all the threads of the investigation in her mind. Yes, she had begun to think of it as their investigation. And no, she didn't really know how to conduct one properly, but she had at least seen how Detective Shaw interviewed people, so she thought of that as an apprenticeship partially completed.

The news about Rawiri, though. That bugged her. Had she really been so wrong about a person? Intellectually, she knew that nice people could have affairs too, but if it was true he'd been having an affair with Maya Stevens, what was Dana to make of what he'd said during his interview: implying that Gene Stevens was getting up to hijinks with some of his female students? Had Rawiri just said that to throw them off the scent? Or maybe it was actually true, and both of the Stevens' were recruiting partners from the pool of guitar students.

Oh, how sordid it was all starting to look. Dana had a small insight into what it must be like to work for the police. Everyone they met must look like a suspect, she supposed. Did they ever trust anyone fully again?

And how should the Fret Detectives proceed now? What was the first priority? If Rawiri had killed Gene then it really didn't matter who'd made the fake guitar, she guessed.

Dana glanced in the rear-view mirror to see Brody snuggled up to his new amplifier. He appeared to be stroking it and murmuring sweet nothings to it. Dana smiled. She'd let him celebrate his purchase until they got it back to the shop.

Then it was time to pay a visit to Rawiri James.

Rawiri wasn't at his flat, but a quick internet search showed he was playing a gig that night at Breezz, an egregiously mis-spelled bar with a name that either implied it belonged to someone called Bree, or that it was named after a light zephyr. According to Brody, the bar was a late-night dance spot where music was a pounding four-on-the-floor background for people to get completely trashed with the aim of waking up in a stranger's house the next morning.

Exactly the kind of place that Dana stayed well away from. The kind of place that made her want to wash her hands after even just thinking about it.

Also the kind of place in which it might be difficult to conduct an interview.

She hoped they'd be able to catch Rawiri as he loaded his gear into the venue.

Oh well, she could save that worry for later. Because now, as she and Brody puttered back to the

Pick Me Guitar Shop, there was actually a small queue at the door.

'What the unbelievably actual fff…flip?' Brody breathed. He cautiously exited the old VW, his beloved newly-purchased cheap old amp cradled against his chest as if it was the world's last Faberge egg, personally signed by Peter Carl Faberge himself.

Dana went and opened the back door for him so he could find a cosy nest in which to lay the amplifier for the rest of the day. After that, he would have to figure out how to get it safely home all by himself. Although Dana suspected that it would probably involve him begging her to fire up the VW again. Actually, maybe they could drop it at his house when they went out to Rawiri's gig. Play two chords with one guitar, as the old saying did not quite go. She wasn't planning on drinking, after all — it was a business outing

While Brody bustled about in the back room, Dana ducked through the door to the front of the shop.

The queue of people out front was still there, so at least Dana knew she hadn't been hallucinating as she drove in.

The person at the front of the line was even trying to push the door open, despite the Closed sign and the immediate haptic feedback of the door refusing to budge.

Dana sighed. Whatever happened to being patient? Sure, it was nice to have customers, but pushy customers were no fun at all.

As she turned the lock she heard some wag further back call out 'speak, friend, and enter.' Which, while not original, was at least witty rather than pushy.

The customers flooded into the shop, and she found herself surrounded by a knot of people shouting questions at her.

She put her hands up defensively.

'One at a time, please, gentlemen,' she cried, trying to make her voice rise above the hubbub.

'There's a lady here too,' someone called out.

'I'm non-binary!'

'Haven't decided yet!'

Dana smiled.

'Good for you,' she yelled back. 'This whole thing about having to conform to society's gender expectations needs to change, and I applaud you for being brave enough to push back on it.'

She raised her hands and her voice even higher.

'However! If you could all just be quiet a minute, I'll take questions from one person at a time.'

The babble of voices receded until she was left

with nothing but the ringing in her ears, her constant reminder of gigs played in times past.

She cleared her throat. Dammit, she was already going a bit hoarse, and with an evening at a loud bar to look forward to yet.

'Can someone – you, sir,' she indicated a random human in the first ring of besiegers, '-- please tell me what this is all about?'

Now thrust into the limelight, her interlocutor was temporarily rendered bashful by the individual attention.

'Ummm...' he shuffled his feet and adjusted a non-existent necktie. 'Well, it's just that people are saying that…. Ah…'

Oh no. She had the sudden horrible thought that maybe everyone was already calling her the Judas sheep because she'd led the police to Nikau. If this turned ugly, what would she do, with Brody occupied out the back?

'What, sir, are they saying?' She bravely stood her ground amidst a sea of potential troubles, taking metaphorical arms, as the Bard might say.

The guy looked around at the crowd, as if requesting permission to say it. Then he turned back to Dana.

'Well, they're saying that, now that Gene Stevens is dead, you're the best guitar teacher in town.'

Again he looked around, and this time was met with several anxious nods. 'So, ah, we all want to sign up as your students.' Someone nudged him. 'Oh... Please.'

Someone at the back shouted that they'd only come in for a pack of strings, but they were comprehensively shushed by the body corporate, who were waiting on Dana's reply with bated breath.

Dana was flattered. But then she thought about it a bit more, and realised she was only in this position because the top dog had been killed. That tempered the flattery somewhat.

But still... she was in demand. It was nice to be in demand.

She scanned the crowd again. There were about twenty, twenty-five people there. Plus the person hopping from foot to foot, waiting for things to calm down so they could buy a pack of strings.

That was a lot of students to commit to.

Well, she could always delegate more of the shop duties to Brody. After all, he'd already instigated an uptick in sales. Maybe it was a sign that she should refocus her energies.

'Ahem. Alright, everybody. If you could proceed in an orderly fashion to the counter, I'll take your contact details, and organise sessions for you all.'

This pronouncement triggered some elbow-shoving, some fist-pumped yes's, and a semi-orderly procession to the counter, where Dana had rushed ahead and grabbed a piece of paper from under the recumbent furry form of Paws McCartney.

With a yowl, he removed himself to the office, no doubt to ensconce himself in his favourite chair, awaiting treats and some strictly delineated types of physical contact. (Tummy rub for 1.3 seconds, scratch behind the ears for 11.2 seconds per side, etc. Failure to comply with the authorised timings would result in full-body commitment to a claw-based assault, Dana knew from harsh experience.)

'Brody!' Dana called out. 'Can you get out here please and sell someone some guitar strings?'

And so the afternoon passed.

It ended up being one of the busiest days Dana had ever had at the shop. She'd heard the saying that drummers equal drama, but was beginning to wonder if the sentiment was incorrectly attributed to the wrong band member.

Word of Gene's gruesome death had infiltrated the local guitar community swiftly, and following on from that, everybody wanted more details, preferably salacious.

Perhaps the collective noun for a group of

guitarists was 'a gossip'. It certainly seemed that way.

No, Dana told herself off, internally. Generalising like that was never cool. People were always more complicated and multi-faceted than that kind of thinking asserted. It was just that…phew, it was a crazy day, and she was tired!

It had quickly become common knowledge that Dana was helping the police as a consultant on the case. Gene's students who'd been interviewed by Wade and Shaw must have talked to all their friends about it.

And suddenly everybody wanted to come and have a look at her shop. These morbid guitar vultures tried to pump her for information on the case, but Dana stayed tight-lipped, and instead valiantly attempted to sell them a guitar, directing them to the latest pointy shred machine, or short-scale indie jangler. If these people were going to be so crass as to come to her shop just to glean tattle about someone who'd been killed, as if it was a cheap airport paperback and not the life of an actual person, well then, Dana was going to frustrate them. And she might as well earn a dollar while she was at it.

There were, amongst the gossip-merchants, a few customers who were genuinely sad about Gene's fate. People who came to actually pay their respects. Those people were admitted to the back room, where they could gather and swap stories of great gigs and good fellowship.

Paws McCartney wasn't fussed on the sudden influx of company, but he wasn't going to relinquish his favourite chair to anyone. Those who did try their luck at dislodging him came away with scratches on their hands and a hissing in their ears. Eventually a feline-only exclusion zone was mutually agreed upon, and Paws settled in for a good nap while people came and went around him.

Dana sent Brody out to the bakery two doors down, to grab a few plates of food for their respectful guests. She'd recently been made aware of the traditional Māori concept of manaakitanga, of welcoming people and showing that you valued them. With the uptick in sales from today, she could afford to do that, and she felt almost as though they were having their own little wake for Gene in the back of her shop.

She was in that state of feeling good about that, at the same time as feeling sad that it was a sad occasion. That odd feeling of 'this is a sad time, and this is the appropriate way to acknowledge it. It is good to feel sad in this situation.'

As she popped her head out the back door to

check on everyone, she reflected that humans are complex beings. Brody, who she'd initially mischaracterised as a lost alien robot, was definitely more of a loyal dog, she decided. He was going round the room, soaking up the emotions and emoting them back to people.

Good boy, Brody. Good boy.

***

Eventually, the customers trickled out of the front of the shop as it got near closing time, and Dana was left with what appeared to be a full-on farewell party on her hands out the back. The tiny backroom office-cum-break room was packed with people who'd known Gene, and every single one of them had a story they wanted to share, even if they'd already shared it a couple of times today. The sharing was getting louder and more emotional, and bottles were being raised like glowsticks at Glastonbury.

At some point, while Dana had been serving customers out front, people had started bringing in bottles of beer to the office, and now there was a whip-round going on to replenish the supplies. This was going to be a long night.

Dana resigned herself to the fact that she was not

going to be able to shift these people on. In fact, she felt honoured that it was her shop in which they'd gathered for such a special occasion.

So she decided that getting the hell out of there was the better part of valour. After all, these people were known to her, and she trusted them not to wreck the place while she went out to talk to Rawiri.

Well, she mostly trusted them not to wreck the place. Or rather, she trusted them not to completely wreck the place.

She caught Brody's eye on her third attempt, as he was ferrying a plate of sandwiches around the cramped room. She was fairly certain she spotted him being offered – and accepting – a swig of something potent too.

When she finally managed to get him over to where she was standing, she gave her commands.

'I need you to stay here and look after the place while I go and talk to Rawiri.'

'No problem, boss!' Brody attempted a salute, only just remembering in time that he was holding a plate of sandwiches. He caught most of them, and then Dana watched as he shunted the fallen ones off under her desk with his foot. Did he really think he'd gotten away with that?

'You're on cleanup duty in the morning,' she told

him, and his smile faded as quickly as notes plucked on a banjo. 'And if I catch you drinking any more alcohol, I will not hesitate to fire you. Are we clear?'

He nodded. 'Clear as a Dan Armstrong plexiglass guitar, boss.'

Dana knew that a plexi guitar was pretty clear, but she still held Brody's gaze for a bit longer, to make sure he knew she really meant it.

She'd seen too many good musicians – hell, good people in general – drink too much and waste their lives away. She wasn't going to let it happen to Brody, if she could help it. She adhered to what she called the Neil Finn rule: two drinks maximum before a gig.

And, frankly, these days, there wasn't much happening after a gig apart from heading to bed for a quick read. It was hard to sell that to a youngster as a lifestyle choice, but she hoped Brody would come to that on his own, in time.

By the time she came back from getting her coat from upstairs, someone had availed themselves of a guitar and started a sing-along.

'Ben Halliwell!' She called out to the guitar player. 'That's twelve hundred dollars if you get so much as a mark on that instrument, right?'

He gave her a nod as he continued to bash out a

country music classic, with the rest of the room's occupants bellowing out the chorus. There were both kinds of harmonies being sung: those in the right key, and the other kind too.

Dana gave a rueful shake of her head as she left the premises. Maybe she should find a cheap motel to stay at. There was certainly not going to be any sleep getting done here tonight.

Munching on a cheese and tomato sandwich she'd nabbed from the tray that Brody hadn't spilled on the ground yet, Dana slipped out to the garage and talked sweetly to her old VW until it agreed to spark into life.

The quaintly flatulent old vehicle conveyed her in World War II levels of comfort to that bastion of self-discipline and good taste: the bar called Breezz.

She found a park nearby, calling out 'chirp chirp' as she locked her door. It was her psychological anti-theft mechanism, pretending to have a remote button for a non-existent car alarm. Plus, she just liked doing it. It was perversely enjoyable when she happened to park next to a house-sized SUV worth more than her shop, and that car would chirp and whistle and go into stealth mode or whatever. Dana just thought it was all so ridiculous. So she chirped at her trusty, rusty old VW in response, and smiled when people looked at her like she was one E note short of a C major chord.

Hey, you had to take your fun where you could get it, right? Life was too short to worry about appearing normal, whatever that word meant.

As she approached the venue, she noticed an old van pulling into the loading area down the side alley. The van had one working rear brake light, and signwriting on it from a plumbing business that Dana knew had folded a couple of years ago. Even if she hadn't just seen it pull up to the loading zone, these two features would have still marked it as a musician's transport, to her anyway.

Good, that meant she was right on time to talk to Rawiri before he entered the noisy bar.

She stood off to one side as people got out of the van. The first person walked straight into the venue even as the next one opened the back of the van to pull out some gear.

Right, so that meant the first person was the singer, she guessed. Not that it was a hard and fast rule the singer never helped with the gear. It was more of a general rule of thumb.

The second person extricated several guitar stands, gig bags, a few stage lights, and stacked them next to the van. Then they grabbed a mammoth speaker cabinet — eight by ten bass cab, Dana noted with her professional eye — tipped it onto its wheeled back, and body-surfed it through the side door. So, either the bass player, or someone who wanted to really annoy the bass player, then.

Aha, here we go. A lanky form unfolded from the van and reached in to fish out a guitar case.

'Rawiri!' Dana called out. 'Hi! Do you have a minute?'

Rawiri paused for a second, squinting into the gloom as Dana approached.

'Oh. Hi, Dana. What's up?'

'Um, I just wanted to ask you a question or two, if you don't mind?'

It was so quick she almost missed it. Rawiri tensed up, but quickly recovered his air of nonchalance.

'Well, you know, I have to get my stuff set up for this gig. Can I catch you tomorrow maybe? Is it about Gene Stevens?'

He started to move towards the door of the venue, trying not to look Dana in the eye.

'Actually, it's about Maya Stevens.'

This time there was no mistaking it. Rawiri froze.

'What about Maya Stevens?'

Dana cleared her throat. 'It's just that, we've heard you might have been… having a relationship with her. Is that true?'

She could see Rawiri scanning the area behind

her.

'What do you mean, we've heard? You and who else? Do you have the police with you, or are you just being a nosy bitch?' He took a step towards her.

Wow, she had really misjudged this guy. How had she ever thought he might have been a decent human being?

'Listen,' she said, 'I'm working with the police and I'm just trying to get the full picture on what happened.'

Rawiri tossed his guitar back into the van, and walked over to get right up in her face, staring down at her. He was a head taller than her, and probably twice her mass, and he was making sure she knew it. 'How dare you come here and throw shit like that around? Who do you think you are?'

He shoved her. Jesus, the prick actually shoved her! Dana tripped, and fell awkwardly on her left elbow. She cried out in pain, sprawled on the footpath, cradling her arm. The guy was crazy! And he was still coming at her. What was he going to do, kick her while she was down?

Desperate, she looked around, and spotted a guitar stand within reach. A cool, detached, guitar-shop-owning part of her brain registered the brand name, and noted approvingly that it was a good sturdy model.

Then, a flash of memory: her and Ziggy as kids. Zig was shoving her around because she'd accidentally broken his new Transformers toy with her hockey stick. He was starting to get really rough, and Dana was beginning to get scared she'd be properly hurt. Then she did something that stopped him in his tracks. Afterwards, her mother said she should never do that to a boy unless she was in serious danger.

She was pretty sure her mother would approve of it in this instance.

As Rawiri closed in again, she grabbed the guitar stand and swung it upwards, hitting him right in the balls.

His eyes went wide, and with a long, low moan, he folded up on himself and toppled to the ground.

Dana scrambled up to her feet again, rubbing her elbow.

'Screw you, asshole,' she spat, as hot tears fell down her cheeks.

'Right back at you,' Rawiri croaked, as he rolled on the ground, hands covering his sensitive parts. 'It's not illegal to have an affair, anyway, you crazy bitch.'

Still scurrying away, Dana fished out her cellphone and called the Police.

'Maybe not,' she replied as the dialtone brrrrped

in her ear. 'But it is illegal to kill someone over it'.

'Whaaaat?' Rawiri groaned. 'I didn't kill anyone. Are you insane?'

He continued to protest his innocence as he lay curled in a ball next to the van. Dana scuttled to the safety of her Beetle and locked the doors as she told the police what had happened. Then she got the hell out of there.

CHAPTER 16

Detective Shaw summoned Dana to the station the next morning. She was actually waiting at the door when Dana arrived. Shaw's arms were crossed, one foot tapping out a club banger beat, one eyebrow raised so fiercely that it was almost crawling right off her face.

Dana almost turned tail and ran, but she'd been spotted.

'You!' Shaw barked. 'Firstly: are you okay?'

'Yeah,' Dana replied meekly. 'I took a tumble and hurt my elbow but I'm okay.'

'Great. In that case: what the hell were you up to? And for goodness' sake, you had better not be about to tell me that you think you're some kind of private investigator on a crusade.'

'No,' said Dana. 'Well, yes, I suppose so. But not like how you said it.'

'Which is it then? Yes or no?'

'No.'

'Good. So that means you didn't go poking around this case which is closed, and try to follow your own leads, ending up with you getting assaulted?'

Dana squirmed. 'I feel like the answer to that question is probably yes, but I want to stick with no, because I think you're missing the point.'

'Oh I am, am I? Pray tell, what is this amazing point that I have missed?'

Dana straightened herself up tall and looked Shaw in the eye.

'I caught the person who actually killed Gene Stevens.'

'What you caught was a sore elbow, and a person who most emphatically did not kill Gene Stevens.'

'He had motive.'

'And an alibi.'

'Oh. The gig he said he was at.'

'The very one.'

Dana couldn't hold back her triumphant smile. 'What if I told you he was never at that gig?'

Shaw did the imperious eyebrow thing again. 'What do you mean?'

'Maybe I have proof that his band had a stand-in guitarist that night.'

There was a pause while Shaw digested this as cautiously as a dodgy kebab. 'When you say maybe, do you mean that you actually have proof?'

Dana nodded. 'Yes, I actually do.'

Shaw stared at her for a good minute. 'Well, come in then, and we'll find out what's going on, I guess,' she eventually said, and turned to open the door.

Dana hesitated. 'You want me to help interview him?'

'Not really,' Shaw replied over her shoulder. 'But if you really can trash his alibi, I want to shake his tree and see if anything else falls out.'

****

Rawiri managed to combine a glare with a smirk as Dana entered the interview room. It was the first time Dana had ever been glirked at, and she didn't care for it.

Rawiri was sitting at the scuffed table with a chipped mug of tea in front of him. There was another person to his left who was wearing a cheap-looking suit. Unlike Nikau, Rawiri had obviously thought to call a lawyer in. The lawyer had a folder open on the table in front of him, and was clicking his pen in some kind of odd-metered jazz rhythm as he waited for the interview to start. Presumably Rawiri's legal budget was minuscule, so it was quite possible that his lawyer was not very experienced in this kind of thing, and therefore feeling nervous. Heck, for all Dana knew it might just be Rawiri's drummer, dressed up to try to intimidate them. No, Dana realised that couldn't be it. A drummer in a pub-rock band would have chosen a more straightforward rhythm to click his pen to.

Wade McNeish was already in the room, having a wordless stare-off with Rawiri and his companion. From the thickness of the atmosphere, it seemed as though the score was currently nil-all.

Dana would have preferred that Rawiri was handcuffed to something, since he'd proven he had no compunction about assaulting women. Still, being in a police interview room, accompanied by two officers, she was probably quite safe. Also, she was bolstered by the thought that she'd taken him down before, and she'd do it again if she had to.

She hadn't even sat down before Rawiri kicked off.

'You made me miss my gig,' he spat.

Don't engage with him, said her brain.

'I know,' said her mouth. 'I got a thank you letter from the audience.'

Wade snorted, then quickly regained his composure, though she could see his shoulders jiggling with the suppressed laughter.

Rawiri's glare increased until he resembled a stage spotlight on full wattage.

Shaw put her hands on her hips and looked up to the ceiling. 'Lord,' she said, 'spare me from these turbulent musicians.'

She sat down heavily next to Wade, pointing an imperious finger to direct Dana into a seat to her left.

As Dana settled in, Shaw leaned across and whispered: 'Any more sassy remarks that derail this interview and I'll have you arrested for deliberate loss of traction.'

'Isn't that for cars?' Dana whispered back.

Shaw ignored her, and turned to Wade. 'Start us off, please, Officer McNeish.'

Wade started a recording device, and Dana got a wee thrill from hearing him do the whole 'introduce the people in the room and start the interview' spiel that people do in the movies.

As per their custom, Shaw nodded to Wade to begin the questioning.

'Mr. James,' said Wade, 'you're in custody today for assaulting Ms. Osborne –'

'That bitch started it!' Rawiri jumped in. 'Came around to my gig and started saying I killed someone!'

His lawyer put a hand on his shoulder and did

some official-looking whispering. Rawiri calmed down, and the smirk returned to his face.

Cocky bugger, thought Dana.

'But we're leaving that aside,' Wade continued, 'since Ms. Osborne does not wish to press charges.'

'She's welcome to try, if she changes her mind' said Rawiri's lawyer, dry as an unconditioned rosewood fretboard. 'Until such time, if that's all, I'll be taking my client home, thank you, officers.' He slapped his folder shut and signalled Rawiri to stand up, but Wade put out a hand to stop them.

'Not just yet, thank you. We have a few more questions, pertaining to the murder of Gene Stevens.'

'My client has already been questioned in this regard.' The lawyer's oleaginous voice oozed around the walls, leaving greasy traces on the grey institutional paint. 'He has given his statement, and provided an alibi for the murder. If you wish to waste any more of Mr. James' time, you'll need to charge him with something, officer McNeish. Do you wish to do that? Or should we be on our way?'

Shaw took the reins. 'I think it would be in your client's best interests to continue talking with us right now.'

'I'll decide what's in my client's best interests, thank you very much, Detective Shaw.'

'Right you are.' She crossed her arms and leaned back in her chair. 'I just wondered what Mr. James might say if someone came forward with information that he had falsified his alibi.'

Rawiri's face was blank, but something flashed in the back of his eyes, and his lips went white. His lawyer paused for a second, then leaned over to his client for another whispered conference.

When he turned back, it was to request a few moments alone with his client. They happily obliged.

'Well,' said Shaw, once they were out in the corridor. 'Shall we go and get a coffee?'

'But, what if they are ready to talk, and we're off somewhere else?' Dana asked.

'Let them stew in their juices for a bit. They're the ones who asked us to leave the room, after all. Right?'

Dana found, on reflection, that she wholeheartedly agreed with this proposition. Let that asshole Rawiri and his slimy lawyer enjoy the hospitality of a police interview room while she went for a nice latte.

As it turned out, the coffee in question was not a nice latte. It was a cup of instant tar from the police break room, tempered with two sachets of fake sugar. The sugar substitute bravely fought a losing battle against the sharp bitter tang of the coffee. But hey, caffeine was caffeine.

Wade indicated a table in the corner of the break room, which had a lovely view of the side of the parking building next door. It was so close that, if the window had been open, Dana would have been able to lean over and caress the concrete, had she been so inclined. (She wasn't.)

'Miss Osborne,' Shaw declaimed, brandishing a cookie she had produced from somewhere as if by magic. Maybe she kept a supply in her uniform's taser holster? Dana had to restrain herself from leaning over to check this hypothesis. 'Perhaps now would be a good time for you to tell us what evidence you have that proves Rawiri's alibi is a lie?'

Dana found that she was no longer in awe of the officers. They did a good job, sure, but that didn't mean they knew everything. And she had done her own thinking, and found out something important. She didn't need to feel inferior to them.

Thus it was that she found herself saying, 'Give us a cookie and I'll tell you everything.'

Immediately a small part of her brain screamed Abort! Abort! That is not how you speak to a police officer!

But to her immense relief, Shaw actually cracked

a smile. She reached down to her side, and dammit, Dana still couldn't see exactly where it came from, but a slightly scuffed and bedraggled cookie was produced, and proffered to her.

Dunking the cookie in an attempt to improve the coffee taste, Dana only managed instead to ruin both items. The cookie disintegrated, and the coffee got lumpy. Mmmmm, lumpy tar.

She sighed, and gave it up as a bad job.

'Okay, you know how most band promotion is done on social media these days?' she began.

Wade nodded.

'Grrr. Whatever happened to printing out some posters and pasting them up?' said Shaw. 'All these tweetfacers and instantgrannies. They don't seem to realise they're just making identity theft easier.'

'That's the one,' said Dana. 'So, one of the best ways to promote your band is to post footage of a packed venue, full of people having a great time while your band plays. Rawiri's band does it all the time. I was checking out their stuff and then it struck me - I could scroll back in time. So I did.'

She produced her phone and turned it towards the officers.

'Whose band is this I'm looking at?' said Shaw. 'That guitarist isn't Rawiri. So what's your point?'

'That is the point,' Dana replied. 'This footage is

from the night Gene Stevens was killed. And this clip shows Rawiri's band playing.' She paused. 'Without Rawiri.'

***

When they returned to the interview room, the atmosphere was markedly different than before. The lawyer looked sweaty and stressed. Rawiri looked, if anything, even angrier than before. Shaw and McNeish, on the other hand, were imbued with an easy, swaggering confidence bordering on jubilation.

'My client would like to make a small amendment to his earlier statement,' said the lawyer, laying his palms flat on the table, presumably leaving greasy marks that some rookie would have to clean off later.

Shaw inclined her head, which the lawyer interpreted as an invitation to continue.

'First,' they said, 'I'll want an assurance that what you're about to hear won't leave this room. It could be potentially damaging to his reputation.'

Wade glanced at Shaw, who took a long, deep breath in her through her nose.

'I'm sorry, we can't offer any kind of assurance along those lines, given that we're investigating a murder.'

Rawiri jerked as if he'd been poked with a cattle prod, and opened his mouth to protest, but his lawyer held up a hand to forestall him. The red-faced guitarist grudgingly leaned back into his chair.

'Of course, we understand that this is an important case,' said the lawyer. 'But what you're about to hear is actually going to clear my client's name, in regard to the murder.'

'Really?' said Shaw, displaying just the hint of a small curl of the lip. 'You're about to rescind the alibi which showed that he couldn't have killed Mr. Stevens. How could that possibly clear his name?'

'Because I've just learned the truth of where he was that night.'

'Oh great,' said Shaw. 'Another alibi. And we're supposed to just swallow it, are we? Does your client intend to keep switching alibis until we get sick of asking him questions, is that it?'

'Not at all. You see, my client had a friend fill in for him at the gig, so that he could meet someone.'

'Right. And this person will vouch for him, I suppose.'

The lawyer looked at Rawiri. Rawiri sighed.

'They won't need to,' he said. 'There'll be security camera footage at the motel.'

Dana's eyebrows rose.

'The motel?' said Shaw. 'You were meeting someone for… a liaison?'

Rawiri barked out a single, laddish laugh. 'If you mean sex, then yes. I met someone at a motel for sex, and that's why I wasn't at the gig. The security footage from the motel will show that I was there the whole time that Gene was being killed.'

'The whole time? You're very sure of this?'

'Absolutely. Because the person I was with got a phone call from Devon Stevens when he discovered Gene's body.'

Dana frowned. 'Why would Devon be calling… oh!'

'That's right,' said Rawiri, smirking with blokish pride. 'I was at the motel with Maya Stevens.'

***

After footage from the motel had been requested, and Rawiri released with a caution not to leave town, Dana was back in the police cafeteria with Shaw and Wade.

'Just checking,' said Dana as she toyed with a fresh-ish cup of sugar-free tar. 'Has anyone actually said the phrase "what an unpleasant individual" out loud yet, or are we just all thinking it? I confess to being a bit shell-shocked by the recent turn of events, so I might have missed some things.'

'Hey,' said Wade. 'You did good with the alibi-busting, so don't feel bad about it. Things just turned out different from how you expected, is all.'

'You're damn right they did.' Dana dumped another packet of sweetener into her cup, scrunched up the packet and vigorously tossed it very near the rubbish bin. It bounced off the wall and rebounded back to her, coming to rest next to her shoe. She gave a theatrically heavy sigh as she picked up the packet, got up, and walked over to the bin. Standing directly over it, she slammed the packet downwards. It bounced off the rim, and tumbled back over to where she'd been sitting.

She growled, and paced back to the table.

'Leave it,' said Shaw, gently. 'Please, for all our sakes.'

Dana sat down heavily. Her chair, the victim of several years' worth of police derrière brutality, gave a protesting groan. I feel you, buddy, she thought.

'So, we're back to square one at the moment, are we?' she grumped.

Wade shrugged. 'Not exactly square one.'

'How so?'

'Perhaps you've forgotten amidst all the recent

excitement, but we do actually have the prime suspect in custody still.'

'Oh, come on!' Dana threw her hands up in despair. 'Are you seriously still thinking that Nikau did it?'

'If not, him, who else?'

Dana opened her mouth to reply, but Shaw beat her to it.

'To be clear,' Shaw clarified, 'that was not an invitation for you to snoop around and try to provide us with another suspect. That was simply Constable McNeish using a rhetorical question as a way of saying we have the most likely person in our cells. Are we clear on that?'

Dana rolled her eyes and sighed. 'Yes, I get it.'

'Hey, I'm trying to help you here, Miss Osborne.'

'It's Ms, actually.'

'I can never remember the difference with those,' Wade chipped in.

'Ms is the one where my personal life is none of your goddamn business.'

'Oh, right. Thanks!'

Wade seemed to have an almost Brody-like level of sanguinity, an imperviousness to sarcasm and scorn. Dana liked that in a person.

Then again, maybe he was just messing with her. She mulled that over for a second, and decided she was okay with that too.

CHAPTER 17

Having had her fill of slimy suspects and bad coffee for the day, Dana decided it was time to return to her shop.

It was nearly noon, so Dana hoped that Brody had managed to mostly tidy up the mess from the previous night's impromptu gathering. As she came through the door, she spotted him kicking some pizza cartons and a few squished beer cans under the counter, which was not a great sign.

Still, it turned out that he'd already sold a set of bass strings (there was only a tiny sliver of a margin on those, but it looked good on the till tally anyway) and a mid-list guitar amplifier. Between the increased sales and her new list of guitar students, this month was shaping up to be one to put a smile on her accountant's face. One day Dana hoped to be making money for herself and not just for the accountant, but hey, baby steps…

She filled Brody in on the failed attempt to stick

the murder on Rawiri, and then he regaled her with some tall tales he'd heard last night. Some were funny, some were poignant, and one was so salacious that Dana's hair nearly caught fire. Get a few musicians in a room, lubricate their tongues sufficiently, and you've the makings of a very interesting book, she thought. Although, frankly, nobody would believe any of it.

'Hey boss,' Brody called out as she went through to the back room. 'That lady dropped off more copies of The Town Tattler - shall I just do the usual thing with them?'

'Sure thing. Thanks, Brody.'

That was Paws McCartney's litter tray liners sorted for the next few weeks.

Paws must have been reading Dana's mind. He looked up from the office chair as she came through. She scritched him under the chin. 'Who's a lucky boy, huh? Lots of fresh newsprint to pee on.'

Brody lugged a stack of the papers into the office and dumped them on the floor. 'Here you go.'

'Ta, Brodes.'

She grabbed a pair of scissors from the desk drawer and snipped the tape, causing the pile of papers to cascade across the floor like an aggressive algae discovering a welcoming, tepid pond.

With a sigh, Dana dropped to her knees and

began gathering them up. An especially frisky copy jumped out of her hand and fluttered back to the floor. Paws, thinking this was a great game, executed a neat and precise leap from the office chair. After pinning the offending publication down, he began to use his feline martial prowess to tear it to ribbons.

'Oh, no, Pawsy, you'll just make a mess, hon.' Dana leant over to retrieve the paper, and something caught her eye.

'Oh,' she breathed. 'Paws McCartney, you good kitty. I think you just solved the case.'

His toy confiscated, Paws had no further interest in this revelation, and he jumped back onto the office chair to immediately resume his nap.

Dana took an unmolested copy of the local rag out to the front of the shop. Brody was in the middle of recommending a bass amplifier to a customer, which left Dana hopping from one foot to the other for what seemed like hours, as they discussed power rating, speaker complement, and, perhaps most important, the weight of the amp. As the saying goes: old bass players never die, they just buy lighter gear.

BrodyBrodyBrody Dana quietly mouthed to herself as she attempted to hold her excitement in. She knew she was probably being immensely annoying, but... by Bonnie Raitt's glistening glass slide, this was such a huge clue!

A bolt from the blue, a gift from the intersectional gods of cats and crime fighting. She went back to the office to give Paws McCartney a kiss on his furry little noggin, to thank him again, and also to waste a bit more time while Brody wrapped things up.

Roughly seventeen hours later, the customer left the shop, sans bass amp but avec a metric jeroboam of information to mull over. Brody was nothing if not thorough in his amplifier research.

'What's up, boss?' said Brody. 'Seemed a little bit like you were trying to get my attention back there.'

Dana waved a Town Tattler in his face. 'Look, Brody! Brody, look! Paws McCartney solved the case!'

'Your cat Paws McCartney?'

'No, Paws McCartney the famous feline bass-player from the well-known all-cat band The Bengals.' Dana brandished the paper again. 'Yes, my cat! He jumped on a paper and it fell open at this page. Look!'

'Ooh,' said Brody, his eyes opening wide.

'Right?'

'Buy one get one free at Murdoch's Meat-Free

Diner. Nice! Evan loves that place.'

'Forget your vegan boyfriend for a second please! Focus. Who's in the photo on the other page?'

Brody grabbed the paper, rolled his shoulders, and gave a sniff. 'I won't forget my vegan boyfriend, actually, thank you very much. But I can see you're in a state, so I'll forgive you this time.'

'Okay. Sorry. But, Brody?'

'Yeah?'

'If you ever say that I'm in a state again, I'll fire you so hard you'll feel the bruises for a month afterward.'

Brody pondered that for a second, then nodded. 'Fair enough. We all good now?'

'We're all good. Look at the photo.'

When Brody finally fixed his gaze on the photograph, Dana was rewarded with a proper 'oooooh.' One that was delivered in a hushed, breathless tone, that came direct from Brody's heart, stomach, and liver.

'I mean, wow. Good work, Paws McCartney, huh?'

'You're damn well right about that,' Dana agreed. 'I always knew that cat was special.'

'So what do we do now? Go see the police?' Brody spread the newspaper on the counter, the better to take it all in. He shook his head and made a low whistle. 'They're gonna freak.'

Dana fidgeted with her collar. 'Ah, well, actually I don't think we will take this to the police right now.'

Brody spun around. 'What?! Isn't this exactly the kind of thing they need to know about?'

'Um, yes and no.' Brody continued to stare at her, his mouth hanging open.

'Thing is, Brody, after the previous time I told them I'd solved the case and then was proven conclusively wrong, they kinda…' She blurted out the rest of her words all in a rush, like a poorly punctuated social media post. 'They never want to hear from me again about any further suspects and I'm not supposed to investigate any more.'

Dana plastered on the fakest of plastic smiles, as if that would somehow convince Brody she'd just delivered good news. She waited to see how Brody would respond to that tidbit.

'So… what, then?'

Dana waggled her eyebrows at him.

'Oh,' he said. 'We're going to take care of it ourselves, are we?'

Dana smiled, for real this time.

CHAPTER 18

Thus it was that Dana and Brody found themselves outside their new suspect's house at midnight, dressed head to toe in black, and carrying tools for a break-in.

Not being experienced in such things, they'd brought whatever they thought might be useful. In a heavy duffel bag they'd assembled the following arsenal: a prybar; a craft knife; a roll of duct tape; Dana's second-favourite pair of scissors; an old torch with a perilously low battery; a pair of skateboarding knee pads; half a bottle of some preposterously luminous sports drink.

They ran over their mission plan, huddled under a piece of topiary that appeared to have been shaped in homage to Tina Turner's hair in Mad Max: Beyond Thunderdome. They'd already scaled a wall to get in, which meant they were committed now. If Dana's guess backfired, they'd both be in a whole shed load of trouble.

The bush they were hiding under had seemed inviting, in that it was large enough for such a meeting, but unfortunately it was also one of those aggressively spiky bushes that seemed to always know exactly where to situate a sharp branch so as to poke a person in a tender location.

'Ow!' Brody whisper-shouted, as he slapped away an offending twig. 'Bugger! Anyway, I was just going to ask what do we do if they have a dog?'

Dana eyed their mission supply bag. 'He can play with the drink bottle while we leg it,' she answered without much conviction.

Conviction is an appropriate word, she reflected. A conviction might be what they'd end up with after this caper. But still, once they had the absolute proof they needed, surely the police would turn a blind eye to any… indiscretions performed along the way. Right?

She gave Brody the once-over, making sure he was covered up as much as possible. Since he'd been following bands all his life, finding black clothing hadn't been a problem for him. He was in black jeans, black boots, and a black hoodie which covered a black t-shirt. Sure, the t-shirt had a huge day-glo band logo on the front, but once he zipped up the hoodie, the effect was complete. Total Brody black-out. He'd even found a black beanie which he'd pulled down low over his forehead.

For her part, Dana's wardrobe did not contain much in the way of stealth mission wear. Of course, she owned the requisite number of black band t-shirts, but on the whole, her style tended more towards the brashly colourful end of the punk spectrum, so she'd had to really dig to find appropriate clothes.

She'd ended up going with black Converses (she'd used a marker pen to black out the white edges), black leggings, and then had completely enveloped herself in one of Ziggy's old black jerseys. So long as she didn't get her legs tangled up in its frayed edges, it was perfect.

She gave Brody a thumbs-up, which he returned with an excited grin.

Good boy, Brody.

Off they went.

They crept through their target's back garden, silent as an amplifier in standby mode. Silent as a guitar with no strings. Silent as a bass player who's forgotten how the middle part of the song goes.

They were pretty quiet, alright.

They tip-toed across the lawn, avoiding the gravel drive and its crunchy sounds.

Slowly and softly, they floated across the landscape like land-bound clouds.

The moon looked down on them as if to say: 'You know I can see what you're up to, right?'

Dana ignored it and crept on.

When they reached the shed at the bottom of the back lawn, Brody caught Dana's eye and made some commando-style hand gestures. Dana had no idea what they meant, and she was sure that Brody didn't either.

Still, they were standing next to a window, which they needed to get through, so Dana got the sense of the messaging. Use the prybar.

So she did.

As she put the bar to the window frame, she belatedly paused to consider what would happen if the shed was alarmed. She'd certainly be alarmed if someone took a prybar to her, after all.

She put the tool down.

Brody gave her another series of mildly entertaining yet completely indecipherable hand gestures. What are you doing? she translated in her head.

She held up a hand. Just give me a second.

Brody gave her a theatrical look of perplexity and an accompanying 'raise palms to the sky' pose. She ignored him, and pulled the torch out of the duffel bag.

Shining it through the window, she targeted the

internal corners, checking for security cameras, tripwires, and kennels full of Dobermans. Or was it Dobermen? Perhaps now was not the time for this particular internal debate.

Nothing that resembled a security measure presented itself, although to be fair, the light from the old torch was as low as a bassline from a 5-string bass, tuned down a tone or two.

Well, that was about as good as she could hope for, so she might as well get on with it.

Dana popped the torch back in the bag and hefted the prybar again.

The window gave out with a low groan, as if it had been looking forward to a quiet night of staying resolutely shut, and now resented having its plans changed without consultation.

Brody held the window open while Dana squirmed through it, her ribs protesting this unaccustomed midnight treatment. She had a feeling she'd be feeling that tomorrow.

But oh! The satisfaction of gaining entrance without serious injury. Mission accomplished! Or well on the way to being accomplished, anyway.

She tiptoed round to the front door and let Brody in.

'Okay,' she whispered. 'You know what we're looking for. Any evidence that he's been making guitars out here. Especially copies of old guitars.'

Brody nodded, shining his phone light around.

As he made his way into the shed, his foot caught on an uneven floorboard, and he toppled forward.

Dana could only watch as Brody fell, as unstoppable as a Black Sabbath riff. He lost his grip on his phone on the way down, and began juggling it, which strobed light through the room, and no doubt out the windows too. He managed an awkward tuck and roll which minimised the crashing and banging his fall created, but it was still much too thumpy for Dana's liking.

If they'd had dreams of being as stealthy as cat burglars, they were the kind of old, half-blind cats that thumped into doors and knocked over the food bowl.

Dana's hands were over her mouth as Brody finally rolled to a stop, bumping into a section of wall which gave way with a soft click.

He looked up at her.

'Did that wall just go click?'

Hands still held to her mouth, Dana nodded.

Brody rolled back towards the wall, where he found a crack had opened.

'Huh. Scooby, it looks like we've found a secret room.'

He jumped up, beaming, and pulled the edge of

the wall, revealing a doorway.

'Gotcha!' he stage-whispered, and disappeared through the opening.

Dana hoped he wouldn't knock anything over in his excitement.

She took a look around to see if anyone had been roused by Brody's circus act, then followed him through the door.

'Find anything we can use?' she asked.

'You mean like that?' he said, pointing his phone's torch to the back wall.

'Oh,' she said, as she clocked what he was talking about. 'Yep. Exactly like that. Wow, this private detecting is actually easier than you'd think, huh?'

Brody, always the optimist, went for a fist bump. Dana was so excited that she almost obliged, but reason won out in the end. She gave a thumbs-up to Brody's fist, as a compromise.

For what Brody had spotted on the back wall was a detailed drawing of a guitar. And not just any guitar. A Draydon. And not just any Draydon. A Weka model, of the early Sixties variety. Next to the drawing was a wiring schematic for the pickups. Underneath these was a workbench strewn with luthiery tools. A spokeshave, along with various other implements Dana couldn't identify, but they looked very guitar-y, she thought.

Spools of fretwire lay about, glistening in the cellphone light like a dragon's hoard. Shiny volume and tone knobs did their best to impersonate precious jewels. A small bin held an assortment of machine heads as if they were lapis lazuli buttons for a King's new waistcoat.

'We've got him!' Dana breathed.

'Got who?' came an angry voice from behind her.

Brody jumped so high he almost brained himself on the rafters. Dana gave a tiny squeak, and nearly lost control of her pelvic floor region.

They swung round to face their interlocutor.

He stood silhouetted in the doorway, so that his face was in shadow. But there was no mistaking who it was. Partly because it was his father's shed they were standing in. Partly because Dana had recognised his annoyingly entitled tone of voice from the police interview she'd sat in on.

Devon Stevens stood there with one hand raised. Gripped within that hand was something that looked like a mutant baseball bat in the dim light. Dana peered closer, then realised it was a guitar neck. Devon was holding it rather as though he was planning to use it as a club. Rather alarmingly so, as though he was thinking of clubbing Dana and Brody with it, and then perhaps disposing of their bodies later.

Dana didn't know how he planned on doing that. Would he attempt to use the spokeshave to whittle them down to a council rubbish bag-acceptable size? That seemed a highly impractical idea.

Focus, Dana! She took herself firmly in metaphorical hand.

'Devon,' she held up her hands in surrender and/or placation.

'No!' he yelled. 'No talking from you, you meddling bitch!'

Why did all these dickheads keep calling her a bitch? Honestly, she felt that it said more about them than it did about her. Couldn't they go on some kind of course where they could learn a better quality of insult? Because, apart from anything else, she actually wasn't a bitch at all. She was almost never bitchy. It really got up her nose.

Suitably riled up now, she yelled out, 'Whatever, Devon. You might as well give up, it's all over now for you. We know you killed your father.'

'I said shut up!' He took a step closer.

Dana had had enough of this whiny git. 'Well that's just too bad, isn't it? You'll damn well listen to me, you spoiled little shit.'

Devon looked up to the sky and laughed. 'Jeez, you sound like my Dad now.' He smacked the guitar neck against his other palm. 'He was saying similar stuff just before I hit him in the head with a guitar. It'll be a pleasure to do the same to you, frankly.'

'Pull the other one, Devon,' she spat. 'There are two of us and only one of you. Once we've overpowered you, we'll get the police round here so fast your head will spin. And then you're going to jail, you evil little bugger.'

Devon took the opportunity to hack out another unhinged laugh. He was really warming up to this now.

'I'm not going to jail, you idiot. I could beat both of you with one hand tied behind my back. And anyway, that dumb kid Nikau is going to take the fall. The police couldn't find their arse with their elbow. They'll never figure out it was me.' A thoughtful look crept onto his face, which, Dana thought nastily, seemed out of place on him.

'How did you know it was me, anyway?' Devon levelled the guitar neck at her. 'How did two dimwits like you figure it out?'

I'll keep him talking, Dana thought, and hopefully Brody can sneak around and kick him in the nuts or something. She tried to encourage Brody with her eyebrows but it was too dim, and even if it hadn't been, she wasn't sure he was fluent in eyebrow.

Dana held up her hands. 'I'll show you how we knew it was you. I just need to reach into this bag, okay?'

'Oh sure,' said Devon, 'reach into the duffel bag and pull out some kind of weapon. Sounds like a great idea. Maybe I could hit myself with this guitar neck while I'm at it, and save you some trouble.'

Dana actually had rather hoped things would go somewhat along those lines, but perhaps Devon wasn't quite as stupid as he looked.

'I just want to show you the clue we found, all right?'

He still looked dubious, but Dana moved slowly, and pulled a piece of crumpled paper out of the bag. She squished it into a ball and gently tossed it over in front of Devon's feet.

As he bent down to pick it up, Dana yelled, 'Now, Brody!' and rushed at Devon.

Even though Devon had kept an eye on her, she managed to catch him as he bent over to retrieve the paper, when he was off balance. She slammed a shoulder into him and he flailed backwards onto his bum, dropping the guitar neck as he went.

'Now, Brody, what?' said Brody. He was standing in the same spot Dana had last seen him. He kept tensing as if to run, and then changing his mind.

'Grab the guitar neck or something!' Dana yelled.

'I don't know, punch him, I guess.'

Devon tried to take advantage of the fact that neither Brody nor Dana had any idea how to conduct a fistfight. He twisted to grab the guitar neck, but Dana kicked it away from him. Brody sprang into action, finally. He rushed to Dana's side, brandishing the… oh dear… the spokeshave. Well, it did at least have a tiny sharp blade in it, but it was hardly a weapon to strike fear in the heart of a murderer.

Still on the floor, Devon kicked Dana's feet out from under her, and she toppled over with a yell, landing on her sore elbow again. She was going to have to get better at falling if she wanted to keep fighting crime.

Brody lunged menacingly at Devon with the spokeshave, but Devon just laughed. He jumped to his feet, grabbed the guitar neck again, and swung it at Brody's head.

Brody managed to dodge just in time, but dropped his pseudo-weapon, and ended up tripping over his own feet as he retreated. He went down with a clang in a pile of woodworking tools.

By the time Dana scrambled up off the floor, they were very much back where they started, except that Dana was cradling her sore elbow, and Brody was clutching his side where he'd been poked in the ribs by a file. And Devon was even angrier than before.

'Right!' He yelled. 'This ends now, you assholes.' He raised the guitar neck and took a step towards Dana. As he started to advance, a pulsing blue light played across the wall. Then it turned red. Then blue again.

'What the hell is that?' Devon demanded, as if it was a trick that Dana had orchestrated. Dana shrugged, and then her heart soared as a siren started up to accompany the light show. The police were here!

Devon paused for a second, then made his decision. He ran out of the secret room and made for the shed door, dropping the guitar neck as he bolted.

Dana scooped it up, and slung it low, just above floor level, at Devon's retreating frame.

People often said that Dana's timing was perfect, and she was gratified to find out that it applied to guitar-throwing as well as to guitar-playing. The guitar neck spun lazily, and time seemed to slow down like the end of a classic rock song. Devon's legs went pump, pump, pump, and like a puzzle piece, the guitar neck slotted itself in between strides, and Devon fell flat on his face. Hard.

'Okay, listen up!' yelled someone from outside

the shed. Dana could hear the crunch of sturdy police boots on the gravel path. 'Whoever is in there, stop what you are doing immediately, and drop to your knees.'

Dana didn't need asking twice. She shuffled out of the secret room and knelt. Brody was halfway down already.

Devon pushed himself up in a crouch, and wiped the blood from his broken nose. For a second, Dana thought he might still try to make a run for it, but then she saw his shoulders slump as he realised it really was all over now. He spat out part of a tooth and swore lustily.

As Dana's heart rate began to contemplate a slow descent back to its normal tempo, a silhouette appeared in the doorway. From the shape, Dana guessed it might be Detective Shaw. The next words she heard confirmed it.

'Oh, come on! Seriously? What in the hell are you doing here, Dana Osborne?'

CHAPTER 19

'We caught him!' said Dana. 'The actual killer. It wasn't Nikau, it was Devon.'

Shaw stood there with her hands on her hips. 'I'm getting a bad case of deja vu here, Ms. Osborne. Barely twenty-four hours ago you said something very similar to me about someone else, and do you remember how that turned out?'

Dana thanked the low lighting for hiding her blush.

Then Shaw stepped aside and Wade entered the room, flicking on the lights. Dammit. No hiding now.

'So,' Shaw continued, 'why the heck do you think we'd take you seriously this time? And while you're at it, perhaps you could explain what the bloody hell you're doing in Devon Stevens' shed, presumably without his permission?'

'First,' Dana replied, 'maybe you could tell me how you got here so quick? Me and Brody hadn't even called you yet with our evidence.'

Wade chuckled. 'We're not here for that, Dana.'

'What?' Dana couldn't believe it was pure coincidence they'd turned up. What the heck else could they be here for, if not to arrest Devon?

'We had a call from Maya Stevens about someone prowling around in the shed. She thought it was burglars.'

Brody staggered to his feet. 'Phew! That was lucky for us then, huh Dana? Saved by the bell.'

'Saved?' said Shaw. 'I'm arresting you for breaking and entering, you muppet.'

Brody went as pale as a goth guitarist after a month-long tour of Scotland in the wintertime.

'Whoah, whoah, whoah!' Dana got to her feet. She could see a malicious sneer slowly forming on Devon's face, no doubt mirroring a cunning plan that was starting to form in his head. Dana wasn't going to let him seize the reins of this little escapade and use it to get away with murder - again.

'We aren't thieves,' she protested. 'We haven't stolen anything.'

Wade strolled over to the window and poked the loose fixture. 'But I'm guessing this isn't how Devon usually enters his own shed.'

'That's breaking and entering,' Shaw chimed in. 'You do realise that's illegal, don't you, Ms.

Osborne? Even for you?'

'Yes, of course, I realise that. But we found proof that - '

Shaw cut her off. 'Proof that is now inadmissible in court, perhaps?' Her tone was as sharp as an exotic cheese. She did not look happy. 'Anything you found in here tonight is now tainted, so you've ruined it, don't you see?'

'But he confessed!'

Devon laughed. 'What? No I didn't, you lunatic.'

Shaw turned to Dana and gave her a very unforgiving look.

Dana hung her head. As she did, she spotted the wadded-up ball of paper she'd thrown at Devon earlier.

'Wait,' Dana lifted her head with a burst of hope. 'We found a clue, earlier. Before all the entering and most of the breaking. Look at the paper, please!'

Dana went and retrieved the paper. She gave it to Shaw, who straightened it out, and held it to the light.

'Well?' said Dana.

This was it, for Dana. The breakthrough that her clever bundle of fluff Paws McCartney had pounced on. There was a big photo of Devon with none other than Ray Cornelius, the woodworking genius that Gordon from Meltdown Music had suggested as the person who might have created the Bluff - the fake Buff Weka. The accompanying article outlined how Devon had attended an intensive course with Ray... on how to make replicas of famous guitars.

When Dana had spotted it, two and two had danced around her brain and merged into an irrefutable, steady-rocking four beats to the bar.

All the guitar students they'd interviewed had spoken of the hours that Devon spent out in his shed, supposedly working on his car. But there was no car here. Only a workbench strewn with woodworking tools. Devon had made the fake guitar. Devon was the one who'd killed his own father. Nikau had nothing to do with it, and was only in trouble now after Gene had taken kindly to him and lent him a very nice guitar because he liked him.

Shaw examined the evidence for a long minute, before releasing a slow sigh from her nostrils. 'Devon took a woodworking course with a guy who makes guitars,' she said flatly. 'Oh my. You've cracked it. Arrest him, please, Wade. I don't think.'

Crap. Dana was freaking out. This was literally the worst outcome she could have imagined. She was going to jail. And poor Brody, she'd dragged him into this – well, yes, he'd insisted on coming along, but it was her idea – and now he was in trouble too.

She looked around to tell him how sorry she was, but… where'd he go? A rustling sound from under the workbench caught her ear and then she spotted his bum sticking out as he rooted around for something.

'What are you doing, Brody?' she said. 'You can't hide under there.'

'No, just a sec… Aha!'

'Aha! What?'

Brody jumped to his feet, triumphantly holding his phone. He pushed a button, and the scratchy sound coming out of the tiny speaker said: that dumb kid Nikau is going to take the fall. The police couldn't find their arse with their elbow. They'll never figure out it was me.

A huge grin split Brody's face as Dana said 'Yes! Brody, you genius!'

She turned back to Detective Shaw, who was bringing her full attention to bear on Devon.

'Couldn't find their arse with their elbow, you say?' Shaw queried.

'Well, no, wait,' Devon stammered. 'That wasn't me. I didn't say that. And it's inadmissible, you said.'

'A recording of a confession is pretty compelling, even if the person supplying it has to go to court for breaking and entering,' Shaw replied. 'I think a judge will want to hear it, don't you, McNeish?'

Wade nodded. 'I should think so, Detective. Us police officers might not be able to figure out much, but I'm sure that a judge will be clever enough to sort it all out.' He stepped towards Devon. 'Put your hands behind your back, please, sir.'

'No!' yelled Devon. 'No way! It's not going to end like this. I worked too hard. I made that guitar from scratch, with my own hands, and the old man didn't even care. He never gave a shit about me.'

Devon seemed to be taking advantage of his audience to have a good old rant about the unfairness of life in general, and his father in specific, and Shaw was content to let him go on incriminating himself. So Dana and Brody were treated to a complete vindication of their efforts in bringing him to justice.

'I made that guitar as a perfect copy of Dad's old Weka,' Devon continued, smacking a hand against the wall. 'I wanted him to be proud of me again, like when I was a kid and he'd parade me in front of the guitar shop people. But he laughed and said it was rubbish. Said that the wear on it was all wrong.'

Brody looked at Dana and gave her a thumbs-up, which Dana proudly returned. It was the clue she'd spotted right at the start, without which they'd never have discovered the truth.

'I'd just sourced some proper vintage tuners, and installed them on the guitar,' said Devon. 'Thought I'd go and show Dad after he'd finished with his students that night. Thought he might have at least a small word of encouragement for me. But no. No such luck. He told me I was just polishing a turd. His exact words!.'

Devon's face was going red, and his hands were forming fists, as he recounted the events of that night.

'Polishing a… grrrr… the arrogant prick. He told me I was a waste of space, and should get back to practicing my playing instead of making rubbishy toys.' Devon's chest heaved and his nostrils flared. 'Then he did it. The final bloody straw.'

'What was that?' said Shaw.

Devon glared at her, clenching his fists, his knuckles going white.

'He told me he was giving his Draydon to that kid, Nikau.' Devon shook his head, and finally all his anger had dissipated, washed through him and left him crumpled in on himself. 'I couldn't believe it. I lost it. I hit him with my guitar' Now his voice was barely a whisper. 'But it wasn't my fault.' A note of pleading crept in. 'He should never have given that guitar to some random kid who took lessons. It's not right.'

'So,' said Shaw. 'You hit him, he fell, and then you decided to cover your tracks by taking a few things from the room to make it look like a burglary. Is that it?'

His eyes on the floor, Devon nodded. 'I was so pissed off that I biffed all that stuff in the river, including Nikau's crappy SG. I was going to go and get Dad's guitar off Nikau, but then when you people came back and told me you'd figured out that my guitar was a fake, I realised I could use that to make it look like he was the killer. I could just say that he stole the real Weka and left behind a copy to throw you off the scent. There was nobody else who knew what had happened. It would've been his word against mine. It was perfect.'

Dana gasped. She knew that Devon's father had been cruel to him, but to implicate an innocent teenager in a murder because of that... it just seemed evil.

Suddenly reminded of her presence, Devon wheeled on Dana. 'And it was all working out just fine until you stuck your stupid bloody nose into things, you bitch.'

Right. That was it. The last goddamn straw. Dana was sick to death of being called that word. Without stopping to think about it, she hauled back and then served Devon with the best slap to the face she could muster.

It was a good 'un, it turned out. There was a very satisfying smacking sound, with notes of bruising and an underlying harmonic resonance of humiliating punishment. Honestly, Dana had never slapped anyone in her life before, and she was now wondering if she'd missed her calling.

Wade stepped in to handcuff Devon. Somehow he'd not quite managed to reach him in time to prevent Dana slapping him. Such a shame.

He hauled the self-confessed murderer off to the car, leaving Dana alone with Brody and Detective Shaw.

Dana wondered if there were nice, comfy jail cells for people who'd only slightly bent the law, rather than broken it completely. After all, what they'd done was for the greater good, wasn't it? Surely the police should be thanking them?

Dana waited on tenterhooks while Shaw paced the room, mulling things over.

'Get yourselves out of my sight,' Shaw growled eventually, in the tone of a bear they'd accidentally poked.

'Does that mean… we're all good?' asked Dana, gesturing vaguely at the window, and the whole general scene.

Shaw's nostrils flared. 'It means you'll be hearing from me.' As they walked past her to the door, Shaw snapped her fingers at Brody and held out her hand. He startled, then realised what she wanted. Reluctantly, he handed over his cellphone.

'There's personal stuff on there,' he said weakly.

'Anything incriminating?'

He went bright red. 'No, not in the legal sense…'

Dana had visions of clandestine communications between Brody and his crush Evan from This Plastic Happiness. She tried to hide a smile as Brody sputtered.

'Off you trot, then.' Shaw waved them away like yesterday's empty pizza cartons, no longer filled with anything she could use. Dana hoped she was wrong about that. If they were expendable, they were probably also jailable.

Well, no point worrying about it now, there was nothing she could do.

Lightly bruised and somewhat deflated, like steamed kale, she led Brody out past the house — at least they didn't have to creep through the garden on their way out like they had on the way in.

As they walked down the driveway, she could see a concerned face peering out the window. Maya, wondering why the burglars were walking free, she assumed. And why her son was in handcuffs. *That woman has a rough night ahead*, Dana thought.

Dana was rudely woken the next morning, when Paws McCartney jumped on her bruised ribs.

'Ow!' she cried. 'Paws, I'll stop feeding you so much if you're just going to keep getting bigger and jumping on me.'

Paws responded by walking up her torso and kneading her chest.

'Oof. Paws, you're a terror.' But she still scritched his ears, because he was, after all, a very good kitty, and a crime solver to boot.

After a leisurely breakfast for herself, and one or two breakfasts for Paws, Dana headed down to the shop.

Brody arrived a few minutes later, and they both wafted aimlessly around the place for a while, pretending to go through the motions, like a guitar player who's just joined a jazz band but can't read sheet music.

As they tidied, dusted and straightened various

objects, there was no need for talk. They were both occupied with the same thought, after all. They were waiting to see if the police would visit soon, and if so, how would they come? To acclaim or to admonish them?

So when Constable Wade McNeish finally opened the door late that morning, they were actually relieved. Whatever happened now, at least the waiting was over.

Dana favoured him with a hopeful smile. 'Hi, Wade.'

'Hi, Dana. Brody.' Wade gave them both a friendly nod. Surely a good sign? 'How are you both this morning?'

Dana could stand it no longer. 'Not great, Wade. Please just tell us what's going on. Are we still in trouble?'

Wade took his sweet time, locating a drum throne to sit on, and picking something from between his teeth.

Brody began to literally vibrate with worry. His teeth chattered.

'Have some pity, please, Wade,' said Dana.

Wade chuckled. 'Sorry you two, I couldn't resist. Don't worry, you're not in trouble…' Brody slumped against Dana in relief. Dana's heart reset itself from an uptempo Latin beat to a more slow and steady classic rock tempo. 'You're not in trouble right now,' Wade continued.

'What does that mean?' said Dana.

Wade cleared his throat. 'Here's the message from Detective Shaw.' He looked Dana in the eye. 'Verbatim, okay?'

She nodded.

'Okay. Shaw says that since Devon confessed right in front of her, and has done so officially now, back at the station, then she's prepared to forget your involvement.'

Dana exchanged a relieved glance with Brody before turning back to Wade. 'That's good, right?' she said.

'Yeeeessss…yes, it is, but there's more.'

'Oh. Okay, what's the rest.'

'Firstly, Nikau has been released from custody with a full apology from the Commissioner.'

'Oh that's great,' said Dana. 'We did it, Brody!'

'Secondly, Maya Stevens has told him he can keep Gene's guitar for now, to be returned to her when he can afford his own fancy one. She also said she won't press charges against you two for breaking and entering.'

'Yes!' Brody pumped a fist in triumph.

'So, in terms of this case, in the words of Detective Shaw, you two are free and clear.'

Dana's shoulders finally relaxed, and she could breathe properly again for the first time in twenty-four hours.

'As for the last part of Detective Shaw's message…' Wade continued.

'Yes?'

'This all ends here, as long as she never sees you sniffing around any other cases. Ever again.' Wade pulled out a notebook and consulted the contents. 'Ever again. Ever. Underline the word ever and say it louder.' He flipped the notebook closed and popped it back in his pocket. 'Is what she told me.'

As affronted as Dana felt by this, she was still immensely relieved not to be going to jail, so she took it as a win, overall.

And, since she was nothing if not gracious in defeat and/or triumph, she said, 'Well, you can thank Detective Shaw from both of us. We've learned a lot, haven't we, Brody?'

Brody grinned. 'We sure have. Lutherie Sleuths for the win!' Dana made a cut it out gesture but Brody was in full puppy dog mode now, riding the high of not being arrested. 'We're basically professional detectives ourselves now, right boss?'

Dana put her head in her hands, but when she finally looked up again, Wade was still there, staring at her expectantly. 'I'm sorry, officer

McNeish. Of course we're not going to get ourselves involved in any other cases. Brody's just having a wee joke about it.'

'Very good. Although…' Wade rose from his seat, and Dana could swear he gave her a little wink as he spoke quietly out the side of his mouth, 'I think you did a pretty good job on this case.'

He swaggered out the door as Dana shared a satisfied smile with Brody.

Before she could suggest they shut up shop early to celebrate, the phone rang.

Brody did a happy dance around the counter while Dana answered the call.

'Oh, hi, Gordon. Good, good. Hey, sorry to interrupt but I want to tell you that Nikau has been released. Yes, we figured out who actually killed Gene.' She gave him an abbreviated version of their escapades and Devon's arrest. Gordon was impressed and relieved in equal measure.

'Oh, but sorry, what did you call for?' Dana listened as Gordon delivered his news. 'Right, yes. Thank you.'

Brody salsa'd over as she ended the call.

'What did Gordon say?' he asked.

'First, congrats on the good result on catching Devon.'

'Yes!' Brody crowed, throwing in a shimmy to

emphasise it.

'Also,' Dana continued more quietly, 'he's tracked down a few of Ziggy's old road crew members who still live in town.'

Brody's wind-up dancing spring wound slowly down. 'Oh. Right. That's good, though, yeah?'

Dana gave him a poignant smile. 'Yes, it's good. It'll get me closer to finding out what happened to Ziggy, and how his guitar ended up at Zander's Rare Guitars. More leads for the Fret Detectives to follow up. What do you say?'

Brody tapped his chin for a second. 'I say…'

'Yes?'

Brody tapped play on his phone, which was synced to the Pick Me Guitar Shop's sound system, and some joyous funky chords turned the air velvety purple.

He punched the air and started leaping about the store with joy and abandon. 'I say… I say…'

'What do you say, Brody?'

He jumped around right in front of her, big eyes alight. 'I say, go the Lutherie Sleuths!' And then he bounded off, singing 'You've Got Me Sleuthing' to the tune of Jimi Hendrix's 'You've Got Me Floating'. It was a performance that was remarkable more for its vigour than its polish, but remarkable nonetheless.

What the heck, thought Dana. And she pogo-ed after him, yelling 'Fret Detectives!' at the top of her lungs.

Paws McCartney looked up from where he'd settled on the cash register.

He gave the prancing humans a disdainful glare, licked his flanks for a minute, and then hunkered down for a well-earned rest.

About the Author

Bing Turkby lives in Aotearoa with his wife and two furry feline landlords.

He makes music with Heavy Blarney and The Bing Turkby Ensemble

Find more books by Bing at https://turkby.co.nz

By the way, weka are real birds, native to Aotearoa. And buff weka is a subspecies. Most weka are predominantly grey/brown, but the buff weka can have different patterning, and even pink bills or legs, ie. they are more blinged-out than normal weka, just like the fictional guitars in the story.

www.ingramcontent.com/pod-product-compliance
Lightning Source LLC
Chambersburg PA
CBHW032004050726